I'm Forever
NEW YORK'S
FINEST

KS Publications
www.kikiswinson.net

Publisher's address:

K.S. Publications
P.O. Box 68878
Virginia Beach, VA 23471

Website: www.kikiswinson.net
Email: KS.publications@yahoo.com

ISBN-13: 978-0985349530
ISBN-10: 0985349530

First Edition: April 2013

10 9 8 7 6 5 4 3 2 1

Editors: Letitia Carrington
Interior & Cover Design: Davida Baldwin (OddBalldsgn.com)
Cover Photo: Davida Baldwin

Printed in the United States of America

Don't Miss Out On These Other Titles:

PRELUDE

It took a lot of manpower and machinery to snatch my brother Reggie from the clutches of Miguel Chavez and his henchmen. When it was all over Reggie, and Damian walked away with gun shot injuries but they weren't life threatening. Stone and my dad carried Reggie away. He had an arm around each man. I took the lead with one of Stone's men and we moved with purpose. Damian was with me too. He was shot in the shoulder, but he was good. The other men were behind us and we were moving to get the hell out of there. One of the guys had already pulled an SUV up and he and another guy ran in the warehouse and grabbed their dead comrade.

Reggie was thrown in the back of the SUV we were driving. We all got in and hauled ass out of Manhattan. We all went in different directions. The funny thing was we didn't hear sirens until we were a good two or three miles away and they were moving in the other direction.

I was exhausted, but I felt good. It was the adrenaline that was kicking my ass. Stone was driving and I was his shotgun. My father was attending to both Reggie's and Damian's wounds. We weren't breaking any speed limits. It was all about getting back to Jersey safe and sound, and hopefully getting the fuck out of this whole fucking area as soon as possible. I wasn't sure if Damian or Reggie would be able to travel by tomorrow.

Stone pulled out his cell phone and called someone I assumed was a doctor because he told the person on the phone about Damian and Reggie's injuries, and even told the caller where we were staying.

If this wasn't the craziest shit then I don't know what was. And I truly didn't realize how crazy until I heard my dad on the phone telling my mother "Code DC." That was all he said. When I asked him what that meant, he told me that was my mother's signal to pack up their belongings and move to Denver, Colorado. That was their secret code once shit got too crazy in New York, the family had to leave town for good. It had to be a safer place. A place no one would even imagine looking. Their old friend, George Hopkins, lived in Denver. According to Foxx, he and George went way back like he and Stone did. So, he was a trustworthy cat. Supposedly, George had been in Denver for fifteen years now and settled down in a cozy spot. He was heavily connected to the streets. And he was well respected by some major players in the area. So, if he needed any favors they were good as done. Foxx took George up on his offer and the deal was sealed.

While we planned to move on with our lives and leave our business affairs in New York behind us, I realized that Miguel Chavez was truly dead and we were responsible. And as crazy as it sounded, it was also then that I realized we weren't going anywhere.

We were going to stand our ground and fight it out with Marco Chavez. We knew we were going to have to deal with him next. Marco wasn't going to let us rest without seeing one of us pay for what we did to his son, Miguel. So, we say, bring it on. We never found out if that UPS driver was a Fed or not. And it wouldn't surprise us to find out it was. It also wouldn't surprise us to find out Miguel was behind the delivery driver incident. Mobsters like him always had a few tricks up their sleeves. Either way, a war was in the works and take my word we would be ready. And as far as the Feds go, we feel like if we stay off the radar, we'd be okay. But if for some reason, we happened to run into them, then we'd rather go out like soldiers than to let them take us into custody. My family and I aren't built for the prison cells, so we're going to do everything we can to live on these streets until the day we all die. I know it sounds crazy. But hey, we lived by the gun and that's how we intend to die.

That alone made my family and I *New York's Finest.*

CHAPTER ONE
Life's a Bitch

D
amian and I had once again escaped death. We left New York with my family in tow. Foxx and my mother headed to Colorado, my brother Reggie and his pregnant girlfriend on their heels. Stone provided two vehicles for them to travel across state lines. It felt really good to know that everyone was all right and that we were going somewhere safe for the moment. Yeah, I said for the moment because I knew how street life was. When there was blood shed, there would always be a dark force lurking behind the scene seeking revenge. It's been proven time after time. So, our focus was to stay ahead of the game and never let our guards down.

Instead of going back to Damian's brother's spot in Nebraska, Damian and I decided that it would be best to head to Colorado with my family. We knew we'd be better off if we'd all stay together. That way we'd have a better chance of staying alive.

Seven hours into the drive Reggie called my cell phone and informed Damian and I that he planned to pull over at the next service station because Malika needed to use the rest room. "Okay. Cool." I replied.

The next service station was about five miles away and after we stopped and parked our cars everyone except my dad got out to stretch their legs. "Going in the store?" Damian asked me.

"No, I'm gonna go and check on Foxx." I told him.

"Want me to get you a bag of chips and a soda?" Damian continued.

"Yeah, get me a bottle of Sprite and a can of Pringles."

"A'ight," he said and then he walked off.

I watched my mother and Malika head into the store. They were having small talk so they were in their own world. Reggie stayed behind and hopped in the car with Foxx. By the time I reached the car they had turned their attention towards me as Reggie rolled down the passenger side window. "What's up?" Reggie asked me.

"You tell me. I see you two over here chopping it up." I commented after I leaned into the car window.

"Foxx thought we were being followed so that's the real reason why we stopped." Reggie said.

Hearing my brother tell me Foxx thought that we were being followed gave me an alarming feeling. I immediately lifted my head up and peered over the roof of the car. I scanned the entire parking lot of the service station. I searched everyone's face that was either sitting in their car or walking around and everyone looked suspect to me. I figured if we were being followed then anyone of those people could be the culprit. There were over a dozen people looking for us so we will forever be looking over our shoulders.

"Where is the car you thought was following us?" I asked after I turned my attention back towards Reggie and Foxx.

"It was a black van with Philadelphia tags. But after we got off the highway it rolled by me and that's when I saw the driver had a family with kids sitting in the back and I knew we were all right." Foxx explained. "Speaking of which," he continued, "I was just telling your brother that we might have to hide out in different places when we arrive in Colorado. That way if anyone gets wind of where we all are, they wouldn't be able to get us all at the same time."

"But I thought we were all going to stay at the lake house?" I chimed in. I wasn't at all happy about this new arrangement. I wanted my whole family to be together. I felt so alone when Damian and I were a thousand miles away from New York. And now that we were back together, going separate ways wasn't a good idea in my book.

"Listen honey, I know we initially planned for everyone to be at the lake house but after giving it more thought, your brother and I agreed that it would be wise for us to be in different places just in case the heat comes down on us when we're not looking."

"Dad, I understand all of that. But I can't stand being away from you, mom and Reggie for a long period of time. I almost lost my damn mind the first time I left New York."

"Naomi, we're not gonna be that far away from each other." Reggie interjected. "We're gonna live in the same luxury apartment building but we're gonna be on separate floors. So, if anything goes down, we could either make an escape or go into attack mode."

I stood there with my elbows pressed against the window seal and tried to make sense of what Foxx and Reggie had just explained to me. I wasn't at all happy about their decision but since I wasn't in any position to make any calls, I went along with it.

Reggie gave me blow by blow how we were going to maneuver during our stay in Colorado. "Since we still have the money you and Damian were going to use for my ransom, I think we ought to get some work so we can generate more money."

"Don't you think that'll be too risky?" I began to say. "I really believe we should keep a low profile while we're in Colorado. We don't need any slip-ups."

"I know what you're saying," Foxx spoke up, "but we're not going to be able to live off that money for the rest of our lives. Remember it's six of us. So, why should we wait?"

I shook my head and let out a long sigh. I knew it was useless to offer my input. When Foxx and Reggie made their minds up about something, then that was it. No one would be able to make them budge. No matter how hard they tried. "How much do you plan to spend?" I wanted to know.

"Foxx has a connect in Colorado and they're offering us some good numbers." Reggie replied.

"What kind of numbers?" I pressed the issue.

"We'd be able to get a couple keys of coke for thirty grand each." Foxx answered.

"Thirty grand?" I snapped. I was a bit turned off by that price. And I made sure they knew it. "That's too much and you two know it. We sold our keys for twenty-eight. So, what's up with this two grand inflation?"

"That's just how shit is. We're going to a different city. So, we gotta pay their prices." Foxx continued to explain.

"Well, who's gonna set up shop? Because picking up keys at that price, there's no way we're gonna be able to sell weight." I pointed out.

"Don't worry about all of that. Foxx and I got that part covered." Reggie assured me.

I let out another sigh. "Okay. We shall see." I commented and then I stood straight up after I heard my mother and Malika's voice coming up from behind me. I turned around to face them. My mother smiled from ear to ear. She seemed happy that all of us were together. But something told me that she also had some concerns planted in the back of her head. So, I made a mental note that I'd have a sit down with her after we settled down in Colorado.

Malika looked like she was about to burst. She only had three weeks before the baby was due and Reggie was a nervous wreck because of it. This was their first baby so I was glad that my mom would be around to help her make that transition.

As soon as I got back into the car with Damian, I ran down the entire conversation I had with Foxx and Reggie concerning our next money venture. Damian wasn't too pleased about it but he knew he couldn't make a big deal out of it. He expressed his concern and I sat there and listened. "You do know that if we open up that door, it's going to be hard to close it?" he said.

"Of course, I do. But, think about who we're talking about here. You know Reggie and Foxx are backing one another so it will be close to impossible to sway them."

"Look Naomi, all I'm saying is that Colorado is supposed to be a safe haven for all of us. Now if we go there and open shop we're gonna seal our fate. And it ain't gonna be pretty."

"I know. I know." I said. The constant talk about my family making business preparations to set up shop in this unfamiliar town we were on our way to began to irritate the hell out of me. I just wanted everybody including Damian to shut the fuck up about it. And why did I always have to be the middleman? I had enough shit on my plate already. So why continue to pound my head with a bunch of unnecessary drama? I'm still reeling from the effects of that shootout we were just in with Miguel and his fucking bodyguards. His men weren't the only ones who got hit. Damian and Reggie were both shot. So to see them get hurt was a very hard pill to swallow. And who knows, we might be walking into a trap when we get to Denver.

Cats from the streets take it very personal when outsiders try to come around with the intentions to set up shop. And those same cats do whatever is necessary to protect their investment. So why can't we just go there and stay behind the scenes? It didn't matter what Reggie and Foxx said, I knew we had more than enough money to stay under the radar. But hey who was I? I just hoped that in the end, Foxx and Reggie would prove Damian wrong.

What a fucking life!

CHAPTER TWO

Team Reggie

This drive to Colorado couldn't end fast enough. Malika started complaining about everything from having to use the bathroom every fifty miles to feeling cramps with every minute that passed. Traveling long distance with a pregnant woman wasn't a good idea for any man. I knew that if I'd ask her to get in the car with my parents, she'd curse me out for sure. So, I did the next best thing and turned the volume up on the Jadakiss c.d. we were listening to.

"Can you please turn that down some?" she yelled over the music.

"It ain't that loud." I protested.

Malika leaned forward and turned the volume back down.

"Can you let a nigga live?" I started off. "I've got a lot of shit on my mind and this music is helping me sort some things out. So, please don't touch the control button no more." I continued and then I leaned forward and turned the volume back up. I was not in the mood to go back and forth with her about how loud the music was. I needed my sanity. And if I'd let her interfere with that, then I'd be fucked up for real.

A few seconds later, Malika sat there in the passenger seat with her arms folded. She wasn't feeling me at all. But I could care less at this point. I had too much shit on my plate to feed into her drama. First and foremost, I was a wanted man. The FBI wanted me and Marco Chavez wanted me too. And the only way I'd be able to stay alive was if I remained focused and kept the drama at a minimum. Unfortunately for me, Malika didn't see things my way and starting crying out of the blue. I hadn't noticed at first because she had her face turned towards the passenger window. But immediately after she wiped her face with the back of her hand, I asked her to look at me. "Leave me alone." She said and tried to resist me.

"I'll leave you alone after you look at me." I bargained with her.

Finally she turned around. Her eyes were red and glassy and the foundation on her face was spotted with teardrops. "What's wrong with you? Why are you crying?" I asked her. I dreaded the conversation that we were about to have but I figured it was now or later.

"I'm not happy. And I don't want to go to Colorado."

"Come on now Malika, we've already talked about this. So, why are you bringing that shit back up?" I barked. I was not in the mood to argue with this chick about Colorado. What's done is done.

"You know that I don't want to have this baby without my mother being by my side. And then when

I asked you would I be able to contact her while we were away, you always avoid my question. So when you don't answer me, I already know that the answer is no," she continued to cry.

"And that's why you're crying?" I asked her. I thought she was being a drama queen. Or maybe she was being hormonal because of the pregnancy. Either way I wanted it to stop so I figured I needed to say something to make her feel better.

"Okay, listen I'll tell you what," I began to say, "I'll stop at a cell phone spot in Iowa and pick up a couple of throw away phones. That way you can make a few calls to your people and the Feds won't be able to track it."

"Really?" she said. She seemed very happy about my idea. But I failed to tell her that her phone calls would be few and far between. Even though we'd be in possession of the phones doesn't mean that we were in the clear. The only way I'd let her use the phone was when we were away from the house. To be more specific, if my calculations were accurate, we'd probably have to be at least one hundred miles away from the house to prevent any of the local cell towers from picking up our location. I could never be too careful. My family's lives were at stake and I won't let anyone jeopardize that. I could care less about how good the pussy was and it didn't matter if a child was involved. The bottom line was that my people were my number one priority.

Bitches came a dime a dozen!

CHAPTER THREE
Naomi Is My Real Name

My cell phone rang twice before I answered it. It was Reggie so I put the call on speaker. "What's up?" I asked him.

"Yo' sis, I'm gonna make a quick stop when we cross over Iowa state lines." He told me.

I was very frustrated by all the pit stops my family was taking. The drive to Denver, Colorado took a total of twenty-six hours but it seemed like nobody cared. I swear I was ready for this shit to be over with so I could take a hot bath and climb into some clean sheets. Was I the only one with common sense on this trip? "Can we just get to Denver already?" I replied sarcastically.

"Yeah, we can but only after I make this stop." Reggie said adamantly.

I let out a long sigh. "Yeah, a'ight. But let's make this stop really quick." I told him.

I handed my cell phone to Damian so he could end the call. Immediately after doing so, he said, "Are you sure you want to do this?"

"Do I have a choice?"

"Yes, you do."

"Tell that to Fox and Reggie." I commented.

"Don't worry I will." He replied. "This whole opening up shop in a city we know nothing about ain't sitting well with me. Reggie and I never ate where we took a shit. That was one of our codes. And now that shit has gone out of the window."

"Please don't blow this thing out of proportion. The last thing I want to do is go into damage control mode because you wanna open up a can of worms."

"So, what I can't have a man to man conversation with your people now?"

"I didn't say that Damian. All I'm saying is that their minds are already made up. And if you go and try to go against the grain and one of them gets mad, I don't want to have to do damage control."

"You shouldn't have to do that anyway. I used to be your brother's right hand man for years, so for him to talk to you and Foxx about setting up shop and not even consulting with me, is a fucking insult. Reggie knows I'd take a bullet for him. There isn't anything I wouldn't do for him. So for him to play me like I'm some bitch ass nigga is fucked up."

"Damian, you know Reggie ain't on it like that when it comes to you."

"Tell me why I had to hear about that bullshit from you?"

"Because I walked up on them while they were talking about it."

"Well, the way it went down was still fucked up in my eyes. I just wished we'd gone back to my brother's spot. We didn't have to worry about shit when we were there before."

"We can still go there and visit." I told him.

"It won't be the same." He said. And then he turned his attention towards the road in front of us and sat there in silence. I knew the whole thing ticked him off so I left well enough alone. I totally agreed with him as far as opening up shop would be a bad idea. But on the other hand, he was wrong when he accused Reggie of treating him like a bitch. Reggie had mad love for Damian. Now I will say that Reggie has been a little distant from Damian since we rescued him. But I think it was because Reggie has a lot of shit going on in his life. He is running for his life and not only that, he's got some extra baggage to take care of. And that extra baggage also has a baby on the way. So I think Damian shouldn't take anything personally. Especially with all the shit we've got to deal with in the coming days.

Put your grown man clothes on and chill the fuck out!

CHAPTER FOUR

I'm a Grown Ass Man

After a total of a dozen stops we finally made it to Denver. I remember Foxx hanging out with this nigga George Hopkins when I was a snotty nose kid. And from the looks of him, this nigga hadn't changed one bit. He met all of us at a sub shop he owns in Denver. He stood in front of his place of business as we exited our cars. Foxx was excited to see him after all these years. They embraced each other and gave one another huge pats on the back. And then Foxx introduced all of us. Once the introduction was over, George led us into his spot and showed us a table. He placed several menus on the table in front of us and told us he'd be back.

Now while everyone looked at their menus, Malika decided to throw some drama in the mix and acted like she wasn't feeling this spot at all. She started complaining the moment we sat down. "I don't like the smell in here and it feels like I'm about to throw up." She said loud enough for only me to hear.

"Come on Malika, it doesn't smell bad in here." I replied.

"Well it does to me and I'm going outside to sit in the car." She protested as she stood up from her chair.

"Want me to order you something to eat?" I asked her.

"No. I'm fine. Just don't be in here too long." she said and then she walked outside.

Everyone at the table looked at me. "What's wrong with her?" My mother asked me.

"Yeah, what's the matter with her?" I interjected.

"She's just being herself." I began to say. "Complaining all day has become a hobby of hers."

"Being pregnant can make a woman very moody." My mother said. She always found a way to jump to Malika's defense. She adored Malika from the first time she met her. And the fact that she's having my baby is like the ultimate gift to my mother. But I saw shit differently. Women nagged men even when they weren't pregnant. They were born with that bullshit ass gene. So, I would only take that shit in small doses. When she starts to get all cranky, I would remove myself from the equation because I'm not the nicest nigga to be around when my chick is nagging the fuck out of me. Give that sympathy card to another nigga, because I ain't the one.

When it was all said and done, my mother ended up getting Malika a cold soda and taking it out to the car while the rest of us stayed at the table. "She is such a fucking nag! I can't wait until she has the baby so it can keep her busy." I commented.

"If you think she's being a nag now, just wait until she has that baby." Foxx spoke up. "After she drops that load, she is going to become very needy so get ready."

"Yeah, he's right." Damian agreed with Foxx.

"Nah, fuck that! I ain't having it. She's gonna have to put her grown woman panties on and embrace her new life because I've got other shit I got to handle." I vented.

"Reggie, I'm feeling what you're saying," Naomi interjected, "but at the same time you've got to remember that she feels like she's having that baby all by herself. She doesn't have any of her family here. So, you're gonna have to be a little more supportive."

"Nah man, fuck that! She chose to be with me. So, whatever I'm into she gotta deal with it."

"She didn't have a problem with spending your dough, huh?" Damian commented sarcastically.

I swear I didn't know whether to laugh with this nigga or check him for disrespecting my lady. I knew Malika was a bitch at times but I didn't need another nigga telling me that.

"Have you thought about if she's going to have the baby in a hospital or not?" Naomi changed the subject. And I'm glad she did because the more I thought about Damian's comment, the more I got mad.

"We talked about it. But, I think it would be better if we can get one of those midwife chicks to help her have the baby at the spot we're going to be staying at." I said.

"You know you're gonna still have to fill out a birth certificate and register the baby so he or she can have a social security number?" Naomi replied.

"Nah, I didn't know that."

"Yeah, the midwife will definitely require Malika to do that. So, y'all better get a plan into motion right now." She continued.

"Are you guys gonna get a bite to eat?" George asked everyone after he walked back to our table.

Foxx spoke up first. "Sorry brother George, we got into a discussion and got side tracked."

"Oh it's all good. Just yell my name when you want me to come back." George told my father.

"No have a seat for a minute so I can run something by you." Foxx insisted.

George grabbed Malika's seat and sat down. "What's up?" he asked.

"How soon can we set things in motion?" Foxx asked him.

"You can do it as early as tomorrow." George replied with certainty. "My guys are ready whenever you are."

"When you say my guys, are you saying that these men work directly with you?" Damian interjected. His sudden outburst shocked Foxx and I. We both looked at each other. I can't say why this nigga thought it was okay to step to Foxx's connect. He was definitely out of line and I wanted to be the nigga to tell him that. But I figured right now wasn't the time or the place.

"No son, I've been out of the game for a few years. But I do know those guys personally and they assured me that they would take real good care of you." George explained.

"Come on Damian," Reggie spoke up, "whatcha' think me and my pops would bring y'all down here and shit wasn't right?"

"Of course not, but you can never be too sure." Damian replied. But for some reason he acted like he wanted to say more. For his sake, I'm glad he didn't.

"Well, don't you worry because Foxx and I have this thing under control," I told him.

After I said what I needed to say to Damian, I let Foxx take the floor. Foxx laid out a few scenarios just to put a few concerns to rest. And when it was time for George to speak, he told us everything we needed to know about where we were setting up shop and the quality of dope we needed to stay relevant. He even ran down everything from how much the merchandise will cost to how the trade-off will go down. Plus he gave us the run down about the cats we're gonna be doing business with. I didn't like the idea of doing business with a bunch of Mexican niggas. With the bad experience we'd just encountered with those other Hispanic cats, I wasn't looking forward to another episode of cowboys and Indians. I was tired of all the shootouts. I just want to make some dough so I can live my life and take care of my family. But when George assured us that those Mexican cats were good niggas, I kind of let my guard down.

During the entire conversation, I watched George's mannerism and his body language and I had to say that he seemed like he was a thorough man. It isn't too many niggas walking the streets that can say that they are thorough cats. The world we now live in is cut throat like a motherfucker. And if you ain't got it in you to take a nigga out as soon as he crosses you, then you're gonna be the nigga that would eventually be put to rest.

I knew I'd escaped many attempts on my life, so maybe my time was running out. If that was the case, then I'd better live my life to the fullest while I had a chance.

Death knocks on everyone's door.

CHAPTER FIVE

Can You Say First Lady?

B ack in the car I checked Damian for that bullshit argument he almost started with Reggie. All I wanted was peace amongst us and it seemed like Damian was going against the grain. "What were you trying to do back there?" I snapped. I was frustrated like nobody's business and the way Damian acted back at George's sub shop was at the core of it.

"Yo' listen Naomi, I know Reggie is your family and you don't want no drama flaring up between me and him. But you can't blame me for blowing up the spot when our freedom is at stake. I'm not trying to go to jail for nobody. For all we know, those Mexican cats could be working with the cops." Damian expressed.

"And neither am I. But there's a way to do things Damian. And that stunt you pulled earlier wasn't cool."

"Well what was I supposed to do? Just sit there like some bitch ass nigga that took orders from his boss?"

"Of course not. But there are rules we have to follow when we're a part of an organization. And one of those rules happen to say that you can't question the boss's connect, especially in the presence of the boss.

Because when you do that you make the boss look like he's weak and incompetent. So, the fact that you questioned George about the Mexican cats we're supposed to do business with, kind of made Reggie and Foxx look like you were undermining their authority."

"I know what the rules are. And I wouldn't have done what I did today any other time. But we've got a lot to lose Naomi, and all I wanted to do was be the voice of reason. That's it."

"Well, you just make sure you tell Foxx and Reggie that the first chance you get."

"And I will."

"Good." I said and then I turned forward in the car seat. Damian was driving so he made sure he followed closely behind Reggie. We were in Denver and from the looks of it; this place had more fields and trees than the east coast. There were many acres of land surrounding us and they were beautiful.

Denver also had a downtown area and it wasn't like New York City, but it would do. George set Damian and I up in a nice apartment in the Golden Triangle District of Denver. The apartment building was called the Acoma Building and it was located near the city museum. Damian and I apartment was on the sixth floor while Reggie, Malika and my parent's apartment was located on the seventh floor. To be more specific, my parent's place was only two doors away from Reggie's place.

All of our apartments were fully furnished and we all had the same amenities; spa inspired bathrooms, granite countertops, European cabinets, pendant lighting, and twenty-foot ceilings with custom ceiling fans and a beautiful view of the Rocky Mountains. It was freaking breath taking. And in addition to the amenities inside of our apartment, we also had access to the fitness center on the third floor, dry cleaning services, the clubhouse and we even had concierge services at our disposal. I was pleased about everything this place had to offer. The only downside to our living quarters was that the entryway of the building was heavily monitored with a high-tech surveillance system. I knew my family well and I knew this would soon pose as a problem for us, especially Reggie. He was going to freak out when he found out that the security office of this building would have his face plastered on every camera. And it wasn't going to be a pretty sight.

While I unpacked my things, Damian told me he was going to go and take a walk and that he'd be back in thirty minutes. "Be careful. And don't forget to wear your sunshades." I told him.

"Don't worry I got 'em." He replied. And then I heard the door to our apartment close.

Immediately after he left I grabbed my cell phone from my handbag and called Reggie. "What's good?" he asked me.

"Hey, can you come to my apartment for a moment?" I asked him.

"What's wrong? You a'ight?" he wanted to know.

"Yes, I'm fine. But I wanna run something by you."

"A'ight, well give me five minutes and I'll be there."

"Okay." I said and then we ended our call.

I've got an important agenda to discuss.

CHAPTER SIX
Love The Smell Of New Pussy

O nce a hustler, always a hustler. Foxx said those very words to me when he introduced me to the street life over seventeen years ago. And guess what? He was right. I was born to do this shit. I've made millions of dollars selling dope so I plan to carry this torch until I take my last breath. Not only did I have a baby on the way, I needed to make sure everyone around me was straight financially. This was my role as the man.

I headed down to Naomi's apartment to meet up with her. Her phone call sounded a little off key so I knew I needed to check on her. I noticed she hadn't been herself since we left New York. But who had?

I stood at the elevator door and waited for it to open. Finally when it did there was this sexy ass brown skin chick standing with her back against the wall. "Going down?" she asked me.

I stepped into the elevator and smiled back at her. "Yes, I am." I told her. I had to admit that this chick had it going on. She looked thick to death in her purple workout bootie shorts with the Nike sign embroidered near the pocket area. She wore a white and purple tank top with the Nike sign embroidered over the left side of her breast. I don't think she realized that her nipples were poking out through her shirt. But if she did, it was a good call on her part because I loved chicks with nice size titties and large nipples. That type of thing made my dick hard.

"What floor are you going to?" she asked me.

I was so mesmerized by her body, I couldn't think straight. And before I knew it, I told her I was going with her.

She laughed. "So, you're going to the gym?" she asked.

"If that's where you're going?" I replied.

"You don't look like you're dressed for the gym," she commented.

I took one look at myself from the chest down. I was wearing a Ralph Lauren Polo and a pair of Rock of Republic blue denim jeans. I was also sporting a pair of leather Prada flip- flops. I was clearly not dressed for a workout session. But my wardrobe didn't deter me from making more flirtatious gestures towards this badass chick standing next to me. "Tell you what, do you mind if I walk you to the gym?" I asked.

She smiled at me once again. Her smile was so fucking sexy. And her teeth were snow white. Plus she had the cutest dimples I'd ever seen. She was the perfect height and her ass was to die for. She had the skin complexion and smile of R&B singer Olivia from Love and Hip Hop and the body of Evelyn Lozada of Basketball wives. She was definitely a winner and I had to have her.

"Sure why not." She answered.

The walk to the gym took less than three minutes so I tried to string my time out with her as long as I could. We stood outside the gym while I picked her brain. She told me her name was Brandi and that she was a twenty-eight year old fitness instructor. But she looked like she was a couple of years younger than that. "So, where are you from? I detect a New York or New Jersey accent." She said.

"I'm from Connecticut." I lied. I wasn't about to give her a single shred of information about me. I was on the run for my life and she'd never know it.

Doing what I do best, I immediately changed the subject and asked her if she had a man and when she told me she did, I was one happy nigga. And when she told me that her man was in fact her husband, I almost did a couple of jumping jacks. Sneaking around with a chick who had to go home to her man was the best arrangement in the world. "What about you?" she said.

"What about me?" I replied. I knew she wanted to know if I was married or had a girl. But I was the type of man who'd never volunteer any information unless I was asked. And even then, I'd find myself telling a lie or two. But in this case, I knew I had to tell her about Malika. The fact that we all lived in the same building was a good enough reason. So Brandi was bound to run into Malika. Aside from that, Malika was carrying my baby and I couldn't deny being with her.

"So, are you married or seeing anyone?" she pressed the issue.

"I'm not married. But yeah, I'm seeing some-one."

"Do you two live together?"

"Yeah, I guess you can say that." I said in a round about way. I was really down playing my living arrangements with Malika since this was the first time she and I shared an apartment together.

"So, what's this mystery lady's name?" her questioned continued to come. It felt like I was being interrogated.

"Her name is Malika."

"Aww, that's a cute name. So are you two ever going to get married?"

"We've never talked about it so I guess the answer is no." I lied. Of course Malika and I talked about it. But, I always found a way to divert the conversation. I had just gotten out of a marriage with my last wife by having the bitch murdered. So, hearing another set of wedding bells wasn't in the cards for me. Brandi didn't need to know any of that. The less she knew about me and the people around me the better off we all will be. "So where is your husband now?" I diverted the attention back on her.

"He's an executive for a software company so he's out of town on business."

"So, that means you're gonna be home alone tonight?"

"I might," she smiled.

"Well if you are, why don't you let me take you out for a bite to eat later on this evening?" I asked. I figured since she had already given me fifteen minutes of her time, that she'd give me more when the time was right.

She stood there and thought for a minute and then she smiled once again. "Okay, I'll tell you what," she began to say, "if you take me to this new Italian restaurant around the corner, then the answer would be yes."

I smiled back at her. I felt like I had just won a huge ass trophy or something. This chick was bad. And I figured that if I played my cards right I'd be able to fuck her right after I fill up her tiny little belly. Fucking a new chick was always a quest niggas like me went after. It was the way of life for us. New pussy was the next best thing besides making money.

Immediately after I promised to take her to that restaurant I took her number and stored it in my phone. "I'll call you later." I told her and then I turned around to leave.

"But you forgot to give me your name." she said.

I thought for a second and then I said, "My name is Jimmy, but call me Jim." I instructed her.

"Okay, so Jim it is," she repeated and then I walked off.

I looked back to see if she was watching me. And guess what? She was. I smiled and winked my eye at her to let her know that everything was all good.

On my elevator ride up to Naomi's floor, I saved Brandi's cell phone number under the apartment buildings manager's name just in case Malika got the urge to go through my phone while I'm not around.

Brandi was my new kept secret!

CHAPTER SEVEN
Making Amends

Reggie took longer than expected. And by the time he arrived to my apartment Damian had already returned from his walk. I wanted to be the one to let Reggie inside of our apartment after he rang the doorbell, but it didn't happen that way. I was in the bathroom relieving myself of some unwanted bowels and Damian was in the living room watching TV so it made since for him to let Reggie inside.

After Damian opened the front door, I heard him as he greeted Reggie. "What's up?" he said.

"Just checking up on y'all," Reggie told him.

Damian closed the front door after Reggie walked further into the apartment. "Everything's good." Damian replied.

"Where's Naomi?" Reggie wanted to know.

"I think she's still in the bathroom. But I don't think she'll be in there long." I heard Damian say.

"How you like this spot?" Reggie said. I could tell he was trying to pass the time until I got out of the bathroom.

"Oh it's cool. I took a walk down to the first floor and noticed that this building had an indoor pool and an outdoor pool."

"Ahh man, I'm gonna have to check that out." Reggie replied. At this point the conversation between he and Damian sounded a little forced. So I did everything within my power to hurry up and take care of my business. "Ready to get back to working?" Reggie popped his question.

I sat there on the toilet and waited quietly for Damian to answer Reggie's question. "Of course I am. But I wanna make sure we're fucking with the right people so we won't have to relive the bullshit we just went through back in New York."

"Don't you think Foxx and I want the same thing?" I heard Reggie utter.

"I'm sure y'all do. But, we can never be too careful." Damian explained.

"Listen Dee, I know you meant well when you questioned George earlier. But that wasn't your call to make. George is Foxx's connect. Not yours, so the next time you wanna start asking questions, run them by me or Foxx first."

"A'ight. It won't happen again."

"Cool." Reggie responded. He sounded pleased too.

A few minutes later I exited the bathroom. Reggie was still chatting it up with Damian, but they had changed the subject entirely. When I entered into the living room Reggie was describing some chick he met on the elevator. I shook my head and told him he'd better be careful not to let Malika find out about this newfound friend of his.

"Don't worry. I got everything under control. After I take her out to dinner, I'm gonna take her back to her spot, fuck her and haul ass back to my spot before Malika even realizes that I was gone."

Damian laughed at Reggie's little plan. I didn't think it was funny at all. "Don't you think you're playing to close to home?" I asked him.

"First of all, the chick is married. So, I'm not the only one playing it close."

"Whatcha' gon' do if her husband catches you with her?" I asked him. Reggie always tried to act like he dotted all his I's and crossed all his t's. But I was here to say that he didn't. When it came to women he always thought with his dick. So, I had to be the voice of reason since he wasn't capable of doing it himself.

"I'm not gonna do shit because he ain't gonna catch me. She told me he was out of town on a business trip so that means she's going to be all alone tonight."

I shook my head with disappointment. Reggie was so hard headed. And he never wanted to listen to anyone. He was the type of guy that had to learn from his mistakes, so this is the one time I am going to let him do just that. He'd learn sooner or later.

After he and I said a few more words about his cheating endeavors, he told Damian that they were going to have their first meeting with the Mexican cats around noon the very next day. Damian didn't sound too enthused about it, but he did assure Reggie that he'd be ready.

"Will George be there with us?" Damian wanted to know.

"Why of course he is. Foxx and I wouldn't have it any other way." Reggie assured him.

"What about me? Am I going on this trip with you guys?" I spoke up. I had no idea how Foxx and Reggie wanted to handle my role in this new venture considering we were in unfamiliar territory. In the past, I was only allowed to tag along and help carry out the deals if I was the one who set it up. Other than that, I stayed behind the scenes.

"Foxx and I agreed to let you sit out on this one. We don't want those Mexican cats to become familiar with your face just in case we got to send you in on some reinforcement type of shit."

"Well, if that's the case then why don't you let Damian lay low too? You and Foxx should hold enough weight for all of us."

"Damian is going to be our driver. So, he got to go."

"Do you know where we gotta meet these cats at?" Damian inquired.

"George said something about having our first meeting at his sub shop. He said we'd be on safe grounds there."

"Aren't other people going to be there?" I blurted out. To have a meeting about a possible drug buy around patrons at a sub shop wasn't the smartest idea to me. In fact, I thought it was dumb.

"That's the thing. We want people to be around. That'll give us a safety net. And plus we'll attract less attention that way."

"Y'all aren't gonna be making the trade there are you?" I said in an alarming manner. Exchanging money for product in broad daylight was a recipe for a disaster. Not only that, those very same people that he agreed to have there could be undercover cops. That would also be catastrophic. To sum things up, Foxx, Reggie and Damian would be sitting ducks.

"Nah, we're just gonna have a sit down so we can get a mutual understanding about how we're going to coexist and make money. And once we can agree on a few terms then we'll get down to business."

"So, what am I supposed to do while you guys are having this meeting?"

"Why don't you and Malika order some Chinese food and watch one of those girl power movies." Reggie suggested and then he cracked a smile.

I slapped him across the arm. "Don't play with me." I said with a half smile. The comment he just made was really cute but I wasn't in the mood to laugh right now. Our family was about to embark on another drug trade venture with some Mexican cats we didn't know, so this was kind of a hard pill to swallow. And the fact that we were hundreds of miles from our hometown New York was scary in itself. I was literally a nervous wreck, because anything could go wrong and I'd be left holding the ball trying to keep my mother and Malika safe. Who knows, it could end up being a scenario where I had to provide a safe haven for Reggie's baby.

Talk about getting the bad end of the stick.

CHAPTER EIGHT
Pretty, Thick & Sexy

Malika had a bunch of fucking questions for me after she saw me shower and change into another suit of clothes. "Where are you going?" she didn't waste any time asking me.

"Foxx and I are going out to scout some potential spots in a few of the neighborhoods around here and then we might hit the bar up the block on our way back in." I lied. If I'd told her that I was going on a date with this bad bitch and possibly get to fuck her afterwards, she'd try to stab me. So, I did the next best thing. And that was tell her some shit she'd rather hear than the truth. I also briefed Foxx about my date tonight so he'd be able to act as my alibi. After he agreed not to answer his phone and pretend not to be home if she came by, I knew I was in the clear.

"Why can't he do it by himself? You know I can go into labor at any time." She argued.

"Malika you know me and Foxx are trying to make moves so why are you busting my balls right now?"

"I'm not trying to bust your balls Reggie. I just want you to be aware that I could go into labor any day now so you need to take that into consideration before you make plans to go on one of your sightseeing adventures." She replied sarcastically. I could tell she wasn't feeling me at all. There was a part of me that wished that we were still in New York so I'd be able to send her ass to her best friend or family's house. Having a chick around me nagging was the worst kind of torture. I remember my ex-wife Vanessa used to nag me all the fucking time. And to get her to shut her mouth, I'd toss her five grand so she could go out and buy herself another Chanel bag. I also used to shut down on her ass and act like she wasn't in the house. At times she'd know not to fuck with me. Other times, she'd try her luck and I'd end up smacking her around a few times until she calmed her ass down. So to get with another woman and go through the same thing wasn't a good look. I was already under a lot of pressure. And if Malika doesn't get with the program, she might start to get smacked around too.

"How long do you plan to be gone?" she continued to question me.

"Just a couple of hours."

Malika sucked her teeth. "You sure you ain't going out to the club? Because I've never seen you go out of your way to get all dressed up with cologne just to stake out a new spot."

"Come on, you know all of us agreed to keep a low profile so why in the hell would I be going to a fucking night club?"

Instead of answering my question, Malika sat on the edge of the bed and watched my every move. She watched me like a fucking hawk. And for a moment, I thought she was going to pour more questions on me. But she didn't. And right before I left the apartment, I kissed her on her forehead and promised her that I wouldn't be gone long. I also advised her that if she happened to go into labor before I got back, to call my mother and Naomi. She agreed to do just that and then I made my exit.

←——————————————————————→

It felt like a weight was lifted when I walked out of my apartment. For the moment I felt like a kid about to go out on his first date and I didn't have a care in the world. I was riding high on an invisible bubble and for the first time in my life, I felt free.

I had already given Brandi instructions to meet me outside of the building at a certain time but when I got to our meeting spot and realized that she wasn't there, I immediately felt like I had been stood up. I stood there for at least seven minutes and then I pulled my cell phone from my pocket and called her. The call immediately went to voicemail and I had to admit that I felt like a complete fool. "I knew this was too good to be true." I commented underneath my breath. "Maybe her husband came back home early. And she didn't have any time to warn me." I continued with hopes that I'd come up with a logical reason why I'd been stood up.

"Let me call her one more time. And if she doesn't answer my call this time, I'm gonna take my ass right back up to my apartment." I said loud enough for only myself to hear.

"May I ask who are you talking to?" I heard a woman's voice say.

I turned around and there she was standing before me. She was as sexy as I remembered her to be, but she wasn't dressed to go out on the town. Instead, she wore another pair of shorts and another t-shirt. "Why aren't you dressed? I thought I was supposed to be taking you out tonight?" I questioned her.

"I had a rough day today. And I'm extremely tired so I decided to stay in tonight if you don't mind."

There it was, my balloon had definitely been popped. All my plans of feeding her and then fucking the hell out of her went straight out of the window. I was so disappointed.

"So, I'm being stood up, huh?" I asked.

She smiled and said, "Of course, not. If you don't mind, we can chill at my place for a couple of hours. I have left over pasta from the night before. And I can make you a big salad to go with it if you like. And while we eat, we can have a nice chat so that we can get to know one another. Now how does that sound?"

"It sounds good." I commented. I had so many thoughts in my head. I started thinking about how fast would I be able to get her in bed. I even started thinking about how this whole thing would blow up in my face if Malika saw me walking down the hallway with this chick. There was nothing I'd be able to tell her to convince her that I didn't have any ill intentions towards Brandi. So, I knew I needed to be very careful and tread lightly while I was inside this building.

Thankfully, it didn't take Brandi and I long to get to her apartment. After she escorted me inside, she gave me a private tour around her entire place. She even took me to her bedroom and pointed out how she'd like to get fucked a little bit more in there but with her husband's hectic job schedule it was a no go. "I'll fill in for him if you like." I blurted out. I cracked a smile but I was dead serious. The way she was looking in those little ass shorts started getting my dick all hard. Her ass was so fat, I could stick my dick between her ass cheeks and it would disappear.

She smiled back at me. "I might take you up on that offer." She told me and then she stepped off towards the kitchen.

"Ready to get a bite to eat?" she asked me.

"Can I eat you first?" I blurted out. She was looking so thick in those shorts that I couldn't help myself. If she told me I could fuck her right now, I'd pull my jeans down and bend her over in a second. That's just how bad I wanted her. "I'm sorry, did I offend you?" I said. I had to switch up the game and act like I cared about her feelings. Women loved that shit.

Caught off guard, she managed to smile. And that's when I leaned towards her and embraced her.

Too my surprise she didn't resist. So, I pushed my dick towards her and held onto her for dear life. "Damn, you smell so good." I commented after I buried my face into her neck.

"You smell good too." She replied.

The way we were holding one another became so intense, we forgot all about the pasta. Sparks were flying and my dick got so hard I was tempted to rip this chick's clothes off. If she was one of my hos from back east I would've made her get on her knees and give me some head that instant. But since she was the top shelf type of chick, I decided to be a little gentler with her.

It didn't take me long to get her to kiss me. And once our lips locked, I went in for the kill. I had to admit that she was more of a better kisser than my ex-wife Vanessa and Malika. Brandi's kisses were soft and passionate, which made me wonder why her husband wasn't home tonight? I understood how the game worked when a nigga needed to leave home so he could stack his paper. But when you were a corporate cat like her husband, you could basically make your own work schedule. So, something wasn't right about this picture. Either her husband is gay. Or this chick got some shit with her.

"Please fuck me!" she moaned between each kiss. She damn near stuck her entire tongue down my throat. And when she gyrated her pussy against my dick I almost exploded. I was carrying a load and I wanted to push every inch of it inside her pussy at that very moment. But once again, I managed to take my time. I knew that this might be the last time I'd fuck her so I wanted to savor every moment of it.

"Do you really want me to give you this dick?" I uttered from my lips as I backed up against the bed she and her husband shared. I knew she and I would be doing some foul shit if we fucked in this bed, but where were we supposed to go? I mean, I could fuck her back out on the floor, but then when I thought about carpet burns, I decided against it. I figured how in the hell would I explain how I got the fucking carpet burns? Malika wouldn't believe a word I'd try to tell her. So, to prevent the backlash from Malika, I pushed Brandi back onto the bed and slowly undressed her.

I took off her shorts first and then I slid off her thong panties. I stood there and looked at how pretty her pussy was. It was just the right size and it was begging for me to run up in it. "Whatcha' waiting for? Come and get it," she said seductively.

"Take off your shirt and bra." I instructed her. I wanted to see her entire body. And immediately after she pulled her shirt and bra over her head she flung them both onto the floor.

I looked at her from head to toe and then I smiled.

"Whatcha' smiling for?" she asked me.

"I'm looking at how sexy you are. And I'm thinking to myself how stupid your fucking husband is." I told her.

"Well, why don't you climb down on me and find out what he's missing."

Without saying another word I took my pants and my boxer briefs off. And before I climbed on top of her, I took a condom from my pants pocket and wasted no time putting it on. As much as I wanted to fuck this chick in the raw, I knew I'd be playing myself and putting Malika in jeopardy. So, once my hammer was covered I went in for the kill. Normally I required the chick to give me some head before I fucked her. But I let it slide this time because it would take her at least fifteen minutes to suck me off and in this case, we didn't have that much time. So I went with the next best thing and that was *get the pussy.*

"Please don't make me wait any longer," she whined.

It was so sexy. I loved when chicks begged for the dick. And in the blink of an eye, I grabbed her by her thighs, opened them wide and then I slid my entire dick inside her warm pussy. When I first penetrated her a spark shot from the head of my dick to my heart. And when that happened I knew I was fucking some good pussy. With each stroke I went deeper and deeper inside her. I could feel the juices coming from her pussy and when I looked down at my dick it was covered in all her fluids.

"Push it back in, please." She begged.

So I pushed the tip of my head back inside of her very slowly and then once I lost sight of my head I rammed my dick in her at full force. "Ohhhhhh yes, that feels so good." She moaned.

Like a master at his craft I stroked her juicy ass pussy like there was no tomorrow. After fifteen strokes on her back I turned her onto her side and lifted her thigh over mine so we could be in the scissor position. I held onto her thigh as I pounded her with each stroke. Her titties were jiggling and I jerked her back and forth. "This pussy is so good." I found myself saying as sweat pellets dropped from my face. This was a sure workout for me.

"Awwww....I'm about to cum," she let out a soft cry. And then her pussy started jerking back and forth.

"Me too baby, I'm about to cum too." I said.

I felt a huge bubble about to erupt from the head of my dick. And after two more strokes I exploded. My body jerked a couple of times and my body fluids spilled from my dick. I closed my eyes to gather my senses and then my body gave out. I climbed off Brandi and laid down directly beside her so I could catch my breath.

"Oh my God! That was the best fuck I ever experienced." She said aloud.

I heard her loud and clear but my mind drifted off to my apartment, which was located a couple floors below us. I wondered what Malika was doing while I was lying in another man's bed –fucking his wife. I was a no good ass nigga and I loved it. My days of being the nice guy burned up in that fire that killed my ex-wife Vanessa. From this day forward, I intend to do what's best for my family and my unborn child. That's it.

Brandi got up from the bed and headed to the bathroom. She came out a few minutes later with a damp bath cloth, pulled off my condom and then she wiped my dick down. The cloth was so warm and soothing. The shit almost sent me to sleep.

"Feels good, huh?" she asked.

I opened my eyes and looked down at her as I laid on my back. "Yeah, it does," I told her.

Moments after she walked away with the wash cloth in her hand, her cell phone rang. I didn't see the phone when I glanced around her bedroom. But I knew it was somewhere in the vicinity because of how close it sounded. She finally answered it on the fifth ring.

"Hi baby," I heard her say. So, I knew it had to be her husband on the other line.

"I'm fine. I was just about to hop in the shower that's why it took me so long to answer." She lied.

"Well, I think I can manage that. And I'll wait for your call in the morning," she continued and then she ended her call.

After she got off her call, she noticed that I had gotten up and started putting my clothes back on. She rushed towards me topless, only wearing her panties. "Are you leaving?" she asked me.

"Yeah, I think it's time for me to go. I wouldn't want your husband to sneak up on you and see another man in his house." I told her.

"Trust me, he won't be back until tomorrow evening."

"Yeah, that's what he told you. See, I'm a man. And sometimes we'll say certain things to try to throw you a curb ball. So don't believe everything he tells you because he may be trying to set you up." I warned her while I was gathering my things to get out of there.

"Wait a minute, so you're not going to sit down and have some dinner with me?" her questions kept coming. Not to mention, she began to sound very desperate. And to make matters worse, I almost started feeling sorry for her. But, then I snapped out of it. She was a grown ass woman. And when you made grown women decisions, those decisions came with consequences. Regardless if they were good or bad.

"I would love to Brandi. But I gotta make a quick run. And if I don't leave now I'm gonna be late." I lied. At this point, I didn't need to be around her anymore. I had already gotten what I'd initially came there for. The pussy was great and now I had to go.

"So, when will I see you again?" she wanted to know. She sounded like she was thirsty as hell.

"I'll call you and let you know." I told her. And then I made my way out of her bedroom.

She followed me to the front door. "Wanna have breakfast in the morning?"

"I've gotta take care of some business in the morning with my pops. But, I'll call you after that." I lied. Tomorrow was the day Foxx and I would make headway with our Mexican connection. So, trying to get together with a chick that wasn't going to put money in my pocket wouldn't be a good move on my part. Brandi was going to have to find herself something else to get into tomorrow morning, because I won't be available.

"Okay, well I'll be waiting." She assured me.

Please don't let this chick be a stalker.

←———————————————————————→

On my way back to my apartment, I made a short detour to my parent's place. I had to make sure Malika hadn't called or stopped by their place while I was with Brandi. Foxx answered the door after I rang the doorbell. "Where's mom?" I whispered.

"She's in the bedroom. Do you wanna talk to her?" Foxx replied.

"No, I just wanted to make sure Malika didn't call her or come by here while I was gone." I continued to whisper. I couldn't let my mother hear me conspiring with Foxx, especially since it had something to do with me cheating on Malika.

Foxx looked back over his shoulder to make sure my mother hadn't walked out of their bedroom. And once he didn't see any sign of her he turned back and said, "No, she hasn't come by here and your mother's phone hasn't rang since I last talked to you."

"Okay, cool. Well, I'm getting ready to go back to the apartment. But if the conversation ever comes up about where we went, say that we only scouted one neighborhood and then we came back in."

Foxx smiled and said, "So, I take it, you made a home run."

I smiled back at him and said, "Yeah, I did. And she wasn't that bad either."

"Well, you be careful. Wouldn't want Malika to bump into her since she's so close to home."

"Don't worry pop, I got everything under control." I assured him.

I definitely knew what I was doing.

CHAPTER NINE
Taking Advise From Foxx

The following morning everyone met up at my parent's place for breakfast. My mother prepared a pot of Arroz Con Leche, which was cooked rice sitting on warm milk. She also baked us a pan of Batatas Asadas, which are baked sweet potatoes with butter and a tiny bit of sugar drizzled on top of it. The last thing my mother prepared was fried green bananas, which of course were my favorite. Every one of us, including Damian and Malika sat around the table like old times. For the first time in years, it felt like we were all a family again.

"How did everyone sleep last night?" my mother started up the conversation.

I spoke first. "I slept really good."

"Me too," Reggie said.

"I did pretty good myself." Foxx replied.

"Well, I couldn't get any sleep last night." Malika blurted out.

"Why not?" my mother wanted to know.

"Because of this dag-on baby. I've been cramping every since we left New York."

"That sounds like Braxton hicks contractions to me." My mother commented.

"Yeah, it sure does." I agreed.

"Does that mean you're about to have the baby?" Reggie replied in an alarming way.

No, silly. A woman can start having Braxton hicks contractions as early as six and a half to seven months into your pregnancy." I interjected.

"Look I don't wanna know about all of that. That's a conversation that y'all can have when y'all are by yourself. Call me when my baby's head is about to come out of the womb."

Malika cracked a half smile and then she smacked Reggie on the arm. "Don't get so self righteous because God could make it so that you would have to be the one to deliver our baby."

"Trust me, God ain't gon' do that." Reggie responded as he ate off of his sweet potato.

I looked at Damian who hadn't said a word since we walked into my parent's apartment. "Are you okay?" I whispered.

"Yeah, I'm cool." He assured me.

"Well, why you so quiet?" I pressed the issue.

"He's over there thinking about all the money we're getting ready to make." Reggie blurted out.

Damian chuckled at Reggie's comment and then he looked back down at his plate.

"Damian, explain to them how we're gonna be the next big thing around here." Reggie continued. He was trying to get Damian to co-sign his bullshit. But Damian wasn't biting. If it were up to Damian, he'd tell Reggie and Foxx not to jump back into the game so soon. He wanted to tell them that we needed to lay low for a little while, but he knew they wouldn't listen. So, instead of getting into an unnecessary debate he decided to take the backseat while Reggie and Foxx took the wheel. "You know it's whatever you say." Damian said nonchalantly.

"Damian, we're a team. And don't you ever forget that." Foxx interjected.

"I'm with you chief," Damian told Foxx. Calling Foxx chief meant he knew that Foxx was the leader and that he had a lot of respect for him. And Foxx knew that too. Foxx smiled and gave Damian a nod of approval.

Reggie and Foxx continued to make small talk. Foxx casually changed the subject and talked about our second day in Colorado and then he started reminiscing back when Reggie and I were kids. He rarely talked about drug dealings around my mother. He figured the less she knew the better off we'd all be.

"Naomi do you remember when you tried to cover for Reggie when he stole my car so he could go to one of his high school buddy's house party?"

I smiled because I remembered that incident like it happened yesterday. Reggie was notorious for taking Foxx's car without his permission. And I always tried to cover for him. "Of course I remember." I finally said.

"Yeah, and do you remember when Foxx threatened to ground you if you didn't tell him where I was?" Reggie interjected.

"Yes, I remember," I smiled once again. "But look at how many times I covered for you before that happened." I continued.

"You were supposed to ride with me no matter what?" Reggie teased between chews.

"Big brother I tried, but you knew I couldn't let anything come between me and that sleepover I was invited to at Mariah's house." I chuckled. "Now if it was something else then I would've held you down."

Both my mother and Foxx smiled. They knew that Reggie and I loved each other and nothing would change that. They also knew that Reggie was like my lifeline and that I would stick by him no matter what the situation was. That was how they raised us. And I'd never let anyone come between that. Foxx brought up a couple more things that happened in our past and that threw all of us into throwback mode. It became evident that Malika didn't like it, so she went into baby mama drama mode. She let out a loud sigh and said, "I'm going back to the apartment."

"Where are you going?" Reggie asked.

"Back to the apartment." Malika answered.

"Why?"

Malika stood up from her chair. "Because I don't feel good. So I'm going to lay down."

"Take your food with you just in case you get hungry later." My mother told her. "Reggie why don't you walk her back to the apartment." My mother suggested.

"I'll walk her back after I finish eating." Reggie

announced.

"He doesn't have to walk me back." Malika said.

"Yes he does." My mother insisted.

Malika was adamant about leaving my parents' apartment with or without Reggie, so she pushed her chair under the table and said, "I'm fine I can go back alone. Just wrap my food up and bring it when you decide to leave."

I watched Reggie's body language and he wasn't thinking about Malika. He was more concerned about eating his food. And this made my mother very unhappy. She was a peaceful and loving parent. She lived her life avoiding drama at all cost. "Reggie you better get up from this table right now and walk Malika back to the apartment." She roared.

Reggie tried to scoff down his food before he left the table but it didn't happen. Instead of arguing with my mother or Malika he got up from the table with Malika's plate in hand and followed her back to the front door.

"Are you gonna wrap her plate up?"

"Nope." Reggie replied as he exited my parent's place.

After the front door closed I looked at my mother and said, "She's not a very happy camper."

"That's because she misses her family. And I believe that if Reggie doesn't let her communicate with them very soon, she's going to leave and go back to New York." My mother said aloud so the whole table could hear her.

"Reggie wouldn't be happy about that." I commented.

"He sure wouldn't. But I don't think she has the guts to leave." My father chimed in.

"I do." My mother interjected. "She loves Reggie but she also loves her mother. And after she poured her heart out to me during one of our rest area stops, I have no doubt in my mind that if he tries to prevent her from communicating with that woman, then she's gonna be out of here on the first thing back east."

"He stopped at one of those cell phone places before we got here and picked her up a couple of throwaway phones." I snapped. Now I knew she was pregnant and pregnant women had mood swings but let the man live. She knew what type of shit he was into before she started fucking him. So just deal with it and shut the fuck up.

"I'm afraid that's not going to be enough. Because after she has that baby she is going to want her mother to see that child." My mother pointed out. And she was right. There was no way in the hell Malika was going to sit back and allow our world to conflict with her and her family's relationship. She was showing major signs that she was about at her wits end with this whole arrangement.

"I know one thing, Reggie isn't going to go for that. He is not going to risk her mother, knowing where we are and blowing up our spot. It's just not going to happen." Fox interjected.

"Dad is absolutely right." I agreed.

"I told him he should've left her back in New York. But he wasn't trying to hear me." Damian blurted out.

"I tried to tell him the same thing to." Fox chimed in.

"Well, it's too late for all of that. She's here now. So we're just gonna have to figure this thing out." My mother added.

I sat back and looked at my mother's face and I could tell that she was definitely worried. She was the type of woman that wanted to see everyone happy. But in this case, it wasn't going to happen. Either Malika would come to her senses and choose Reggie or it was going to be extreme chaos when it was all said and done.

I just hope when she blows the whistle on him, he's ready.

CHAPTER TEN
Didn't See This Shit Coming

Malika walked ahead of me after we left my parents apartment. Can you please slow down? I asked her. But she kept walking. She was acting like the spoiled bitch I made her to be.

When we walked onto the elevator I was somewhat shocked that Brandie would be accompanying us. She was once again dressed in her workout clothes and they were sweaty so I knew she had just left the gym and was on her way back to her apartment.

She smiled at me and she spoke to both of us. Boy was I feeling awkward, but I didn't let that deter me from speaking back to her. After the elevator door closed behind Malika, I tried to act as if Brandy wasn't standing there.

I did however stare at her out the corner of my eye and the facial expression she had gave me a clear indication that she was enjoying this awkward situation.

All I could think about was what if this chick just lost her mind and started running off at the mouth and tell Malika about how I came to her apartment and fucked her.

I mean, this would be her perfect opportunity to rat me out. How else could she pay me back for running out on her last night? And I hadn't called her like I had promised. I knew I was looking like a piece of shit in her eyes. I just hoped that she had sense enough not to blow up our spot, because if she did, I'd truly make that bitch pay.

Finally, her floor came 1st. I was so happy and relieved that she didn't open her mouth while she was around Malika. And as soon as the door closed, it felt like a heavy load was lifted off my shoulders.

Immediately after the elevator door closed and the elevator moved, Malika looked back at me like she wanted to spit fire at me. "I saw you look at that bitch's ass when she got off the elevator."

Caught off guard by her comment, I thought back to when Brandy had walked away and asked myself had I really looked at her. And when I realized that I hadn't, I told Malika she was seeing things.

"Don't play with my intelligence! I know what I saw." She snapped.

"You're bugging out. I didn't look at her."

"Yes you did. So stop lying." she continued.

"I swear I didn't." I told her. I knew I wasn't the most honest nigga. But I was telling the truth this time.

Unfortunately for me, she turned a deaf ear to everything I tried to say to her. Women were some strange ass creatures. I noticed that when I told them a lie they believed me and asked no questions. But when I told them the truth, I'm always being called a liar and that I wasn't shit. What can I say? You win some, then you lose some.

When the elevator dropped us off to our floor, Malika stormed off like her fucking mind was going bad. I let her walk ahead of me. And when we got inside of the apartment I placed her food down on the kitchen table and then I turned around and headed back to the front door. "So, you're just gonna leave me in the house just like that?" she barked.

My back was turned to her but I knew she was giving me the look that would kill. "I'll be back." I told her and walked out of the apartment as quickly as I could.

All I wanted to do was get back to my parent's apartment, finish eating my food and then get ready to go and talk to this new connect George had set up for me and Foxx. I didn't have time for anything else.

"When are you going to let me call my mother?" she yelled from where she was standing.

I ignored her and closed the door. Seconds later, the front door to our apartment had opened and Malika unleashed the beast. "You can ignore me all you want. But if you don't let me call my mother by the end of the day, I'm leaving." She threatened.

I was standing in the hallway waiting on the elevator when she screamed at me and by the time I turned around to address her stupid ass, she had already closed the door.

I swear I was fucking furious. I wanted to march back down to the apartment and smack the hell out of her for that dope fiend move she just made. She knew

I wanted to keep a low profile while we were here. I could care less about her fucking ultimatum. I had already made up my mind that I was going to let her talk to her family when I felt the time was right. So, for her to show her ass like she just did was unacceptable and she will be dealt with when I get back.

I was the fucking king of that castle!

CHAPTER ELEVEN

What Just Happened?

I decided to chill at my parent's apartment while Foxx, Reggie and Damian made their run. I stood on the balcony of the living room just to soak in the air. The streets were pretty busy so there were a lot of things to look at. One thing in particular struck me by surprise and I immediately became speechless. "Mom, come here for a minute," I yelled from the terrace.

My mother was in the kitchen cleaning up so it didn't take her long to join me. "What's the matter?" she asked me.

"Look down at the other side of the street. Isn't that Malika talking to that black lady with the red shirt on?" I pointed out.

My mother took a second as she looked down towards the street. "Oh my God! That is her." She finally said as she turned to look at me. "What do you think she's doing?" my mother continued.

"I don't know.

"Wait, it looks like the woman is handing her a cell phone." My mother said.

Seeing the same thing my mother saw, my heart started racing. Why in the world was that lady handing Malika a cell phone? And was Malika really going to use it?

My mother and I both stood there on the terrace and watched to see exactly what she was about to do. Anxiety slowly crept into my body and nearly consumed me as I watched Malika key in the numbers on the phone pad and then place it to her ear.

"Oh my God she's really using that lady's phone." My mother pointed out.

I couldn't say a word. I was totally in shock. And the first thing that came to my mind was she was trying to reach out to her family. I understood her frustration but this was not the right way to go about it. And when Reggie finds out about it, God knows what he is liable to do.

"What do you think we should do?" My mother questioned me. She and I both felt helpless. There was absolutely nothing we could do about what was going on.

I could run down to the first floor and try to run interference on the phone call, but by the time I make it to her it would be too late.

"I think we should get Reggie on the phone right now." I suggested.

"Do you think that's a good idea?" she continued.

"Not really. But what else can we do?"

"I don't know." My mother said and threw her arms up. "Let's just pray that we're over reacting and that she's not using that phone to call her family."

"Come on mom, let's be real here. Why else would a pregnant woman who's less than two weeks due take a walk outside and ask a perfect stranger to use their phone? Malika blatantly took that walk in hopes that she'd get to sneak a call to her mother and we wouldn't find out about it."

"Well if she thought that we weren't going to find out then she was wrong."

"Mom that's beside the point. Malika is clearly thinking about nobody but herself. She knows that the Feds are looking for us. She also knows that if we ever get picked up Reggie alone would be facing twenty years in prison. So if her careless behavior gets us jammed up, I know for a fact that Reggie is going to go off on her."

"Naomi, you know I don't like talking about stuff like that. The last thing I want to hear is that my son is putting his hands on a woman. So let's just hope for the best and leave this subject alone." My mother said and she walked off. I could tell she was getting upset. It bothered her that her two children could possibly be getting picked up by the Fed because of Malika's stupidity. It also bothered her for any of us to talk about violence around her. So I gave her space and let her go off into her room.

A minute or so later I began to have all kinds of crazy thoughts going through my head. First I thought about how she could rat us out and blow up our spot. This would devastate our family and our freedom. Not only will her actions send us to prison for a very long time, it could damage our family unit. With the type of time the FEDS are handing out these days, Reggie and I could die in there and we wouldn't be able to do anything about it.

Realizing that I could possibly stop this catastrophe from happening, I dashed out of my parent's apartment and rushed down to the first floor. As I walked through the lobby I could see Malika's silhouette through the glass doors. And as I approached both of them, my heart started pounding uncontrollably. With as much force as I could muster up, I pushed one of the glass doors open and made my way outside. Within seconds, I saw Malika with her back to me. So as I approached her she had already given the woman her phone back and was thanking her for her generosity. "Oh it's okay," I heard the woman say and then she started walking about.

I couldn't hold my peace any longer and I unleashed the beast. "What the fuck were you doing with that lady's cell phone?" I barked. I was really pissed off with Malika and I wanted her to know it.

She gave me the typical deer in the headlights expression. It was a clear indication that she knew she was busted. But what pissed me off more was that she tried to act like she hadn't done anything wrong. "Whatcha' talking about?" She asked.

Malika was cool when Reggie first started screwing around with her. I remember when they first met and I remember him putting her up in a midtown apartment only one month after the affair started. He basically took her from nothing and gave her the world. And not too long after that, she became this money hungry bitch like his dead wife Vanessa. So I could definitely see her selling him out for a couple of dollars so she could make ends meet after she returned to New York. I could also see Reggie hurting her badly if she did just that. It could even get deadly.

"Malika don't play games with me. I saw you using that lady's cell phone. So, tell me who you were calling?" I roared as I stood before her.

Malika's pregnant stomach was bulging from her maternity short. She literally looked like she was about to pop at any moment.

"I wasn't calling anyone," she said.

"Well if you weren't calling anyone then why the hell were you using that lady's phone?"

"I wasn't using her phone." Malika insisted as she stood there before me.

I swear I wanted to grab her by the collar and rough her up a little bit. But I held my composure and stared straight at her face just to let her know how serious I was.

"Malika I was standing on my parents' terrace and I saw you take that lady's cell phone from her and use it. So if you're gonna stand here and lie in my face and tell me that you didn't have her phone, I promise I will make your life a living hell after I get through with you."

"So what are you threatening me now?" Malika stood head-to-head with me. She gave me this impression that she wasn't about to back down from me. But I wasn't about to back down from her either.

"Malika you can stand here and lie to me until your face turns blue, but I saw you take that woman's phone, dial a number and then I saw you put it to your ear. So if you want to play dumb and try to make me look like I'm crazy then so be it. But I guarantee you that when Reggie finds out about this little stunt, he's not gonna be too happy with you." I replied sarcastically.

"Do you think I even care?"

"If you do, then you're a bigger fool than I thought."

"Oh so now I'm a fool?"

"Listen Malika, I'm not gonna keep going back and forth with you."

"So why are you still standing here?"

"You know what? Fuck you! I hope my brother tears your fucking head off when he finds out what his baby mama did." I roared and then I stormed off.

I headed back to the apartment building and instead of going back to my parents' place I went to my place instead. I went into my bedroom where my cell phone was and grabbed it from the dresser. I held it in my hand for a moment trying to figure out how to break the bad news of Malika's reckless behavior to Reggie.

While I was standing there contemplating I got a knock on my front door. I hesitated for a second because I knew it couldn't be anyone but Malika's dumb ass but when I heard my mother's voice, I rushed to the door and opened it.

"Hey baby, I need you to come to my place with me." She said. Her face looked weary.

"Mom, what's wrong?" I asked her as she pulled me from my apartment.

"I'll explain it to you when we get back to my place." She replied.

With my cell phone in my left hand and her hand clutching my right hand, I followed her to her apartment.

I swear I didn't know what to think during the walk back to my parents' place. I asked her a couple of times on the elevator ride what was waiting back at her place but she shushed me every time I opened my mouth. I realized that I was wasting my breath talking to her so I dropped the subject.

The second we entered into her apartment I became more anxious to find out what my mother was so secretive about. And when I turned the corner and entered into the kitchen I came face-to-face with this secret of my mother's. I was displeased to say the least. And my facial expression showed it. "So, you brought me here to look in her face?" I asked my mother, as I was referring to Malika.

My mother took two steps ahead of me and pulled a chair from the table. "Have a seat baby," she instructed me.

After I sat down my mother began the talking. "I brought you here so the three of us could talk about what happened earlier."

"But I have nothing to say." I interjected.

KIKI SWINSON

"Baby, just be quiet a minute and let me finish saying what I have to say. Now, I know about that little pow-wow you and Malika had outside. And that was unfortunate, but guess what, we are going to sit here and resolve this matter right now so that we don't have to bring your brother and your father into this."

"But mom how can it be resolved when the damage has been done? You and I both saw her take the phone from that lady and use it. But when I approached her about it, she got all cocky with me and lied to my face that she even had the lady's phone. Not to mention, when she made that call to God knows who, she put our entire family in danger."

"How did I put your family in danger when I only called my best friend?"

"Bitch shut up! You told me you didn't have that lady's phone. And now you're standing here telling me you did have it. So, which one is it?"

"First off, I'm not a bitch!" Malika disputed.

"Girl please, just answer the damn question!" I pressed the issue. She needed to be exposed.

"Naomi, she told me she called her best friend and the only reason why she lied to you when you approached her was because she knew that you would not have believed her."

"She's right about that because her lying ass doesn't have any friends."

"You don't know what I have." Malika argued.

"Alright ladies! Fussing back-and-forth isn't going to get us anywhere. So let's sit here like adults and work this thing out."

"Come on mom, let's get real! You know she is wasting our time. So I can't sit here and pretend like I'm okay. She lied to me and I can't get over that."

"Can you just shut up for once and let your mother talk?"

"Why don't you make me shut up!" I roared. I dared her. I wanted to see if she had the nerve to make me close my mouth.

Malika laughed like she found what I was saying funny.

"You think it's funny, huh? I'll give your pregnant ass something to really laugh about." I threatened.

Malika stood to her feet like she wanted to go toe to toe with me. I mean she literally stepped from the table and invited me to a brawl. And that's when I laughed. So you really got a set of balls, huh?"

"Touch me and I'll show you." She shot back.

"Girl, if you don't sit your pregnant ass down, I'm gonna send your ass in labor for real."

"Do it then!" She snapped.

My mother saw that her little plan wasn't working so she stepped between Malika and I. "All right, now this behavior isn't going to be tolerated in my house. So you two better act like you got some sense because I'm not going to take much more of this."

"She's the one that got out of the chair." I pointed out.

"Yeah, but you threatened me and you called me a liar!"

"That's because you are."

"Whatever Naomi, you don't know shit about me. So please stop acting like you do."

"I know enough to know that you don't love my brother like you claim you do."

"You don't know shit about my feelings concerning Reggie. And besides that, how can you even make comments about my relationship when you never really had one. I heard about all those big time drug dealers you used to fuck so that you and Reggie could get good prices on their dope."

Taken aback by Malika's statement I had to regroup. But before I could get myself together I had to look at my mother's expression to see if she was all right. The comments Malika had just made would seem true if you hadn't known first hand how I worked my magic when I met cats that had access to tons of product. There was no question that I knew a lot of big time ballers. But see what Malika failed to mention was that I didn't have to fuck all of them. Most of them just wanted my company. They had plenty of women that they used for sex. I was more like a business partner and arm candy. So for her to stand here and run her mouth to my mother was beyond disrespect in my eyes. And I couldn't let her get away with it.

As I prepared myself to read this bitch her rights, my mother stepped towards me and placed her right hand across my chest. "Please let it go," she begged me softly. Her voice was barely a whisper. And when she spoke in this tone, I knew she was very serious and she was at her breaking point. And as much as I wanted to vindicate myself from Malika's accusations, I knew I couldn't for the sake of my mother's sanity. She was tired of the bickering so I had to be the bigger person and let it go.

Instead of releasing my wrath on Malika, I shook my head with disgust because I saw right through her. She was an opportunist in the beginning and nothing has changed.

"You can shake your head all you want to, but just know that you can't come between me and my man." She roared.

I stood up from the table because I refused to listen to this crap any longer. "I'll never try to come between you and my brother because he's going to find out who he's dealing with on his own."

"Naomi, where are you going honey?" My mother asked

"I'm going back to my place where I don't have to hear a bunch of lies."

"Bye. Carry your ass!"

I looked at Malika once more before I turned to leave. "You are so lucky my mother is standing here with us. Because I've got a ton of shit to say to you and it wouldn't be a pretty sight around here once I'm done with you."

"Don't talk about it. Be about it! Say whatcha' gotta say. I'm a grown ass woman and so I can handle mines."

"Drop it right now, Malika. I've heard enough!" My mother instructed her.

Instead of making another comment, I left my mother's apartment and returned to my own place. It was better this way because if I hadn't left then it would've gotten really ugly. Besides that, I've got enough shit to deal with on my own.

Immediately after I entered back into my apartment I sat down on my living room sofa and thought about everything that was said between Malika and I. I even thought about the doors that she possibly opened. Best friend my ass! She called her mother. And if my suspicions were in fact correct then something was about to go down. I just hoped that my brother saw it before it was too late.

Thank God Foxx and my mother aren't wanted!

CHAPTER TWELVE

N.Y. State Of Mind

Foxx and I sat at the back table of the sub shop with two of George's Mexican connection while Damian waited for us in the car. George had a few of his customer's sitting at tables on the other side of the shop to prevent them from eavesdropping on our conversation. To make this meeting look more like a legit business meeting, every so often George would refill the cups we had sitting in front of us with more coffee and hot tea. Both men looked to be in their mid to late thirties. And they acted like they meant business too. The first guy's name was Angel. And the second guy's name was Ernesto. They were cousins and they were a part of the Zalazar cartel. They spoke really good English and they referred to us as their new friends. But they drove a hard bargain when it came to the prices of their coke.

They quoted us thirty grand per kilo. And to stay at that price we had to guarantee them that they would be our only supplier. But guaranteeing them to be our only supplier wasn't the issue. Their prices were.

"Angel why don't you and Ernesto consider giving us a better price then thirty grand?"

"Thirty grand is a good price my friend. And we give you that price because George says that you are his family." Angel stated.

"And we appreciate that," Foxx chimed in. "But we aren't in the best situation right now to pay you guys the money you're asking for."

"So name your price." Angel said.

Foxx thought for a minute and then he said, "if you guys can give us a kilo for twenty-five we can close the deal."

"We have premium stuff. We control all the traffic going in and out of Pikes Peak, Boulder and Denver. So everyone who has dealt with us knows that our product is ninety percent pure. So you see my friend thirty grand is a steal."

"I'm not doubting the purity of your product. All I'm saying is that we can only bring twenty-five to the table."

Angel looked at this cousin Ernesto. They locked eyes for a couple of seconds and when Ernesto gave Angel a head nod Angel turned back towards Foxx and said, "we'll give it to you for that price under the condition that you buy four kilos a week."

Foxx smiled. "Sounds like you got yourself a deal."

Both men smiled back at Foxx. But I wasn't too happy about the deal. Copping four bricks a week was an insane idea. Because for one we didn't have a clientele and two, it would be too risky to hold that much coke in our possession especially while we were on the run. And as much as I wanted to shut down the deal, I remained tight lipped. Foxx had to have had a plan when he agreed to those conditions. I guessed in time I'd hear all about it.

"When will you be prepared to make our first trade-off?" Fox asked.

"We can do it as early as tonight." Angel replied.

"Okay. Let's make it happen." Fox told them.

Ernesto and Angel stood up from the table and shook me and Foxx's hands. We'll be in touch with George. He'll know the time and the location." Angel concluded.

"Okay. Great." Foxx said.

"Foxx please tell me why you agreed to off load four kilos a week from them?" I asked. I needed some answers.

"Don't worry son. I've got everything under control."

"I'm sure you do. But we don't have the clientele or a street team to distribute the product to."

"We will by tomorrow," he assured me. And then he walked over to the other side of the sub shop where George was standing.

Let the games begin!

CHAPTER THIRTEEN
Eye For An Eye

It seemed like Damian had been gone away for hours. So when he returned back to the apartment I had a ton of shit to tell him.

When he saw me laying on the bed watching television he sat on the bed next to me and asked me what I had been doing while he was out.

You will not believe the shit that happened while you guys were gone.

"I'm all ears," he said.

I sat up in the bed and went into the spiel about the argument I had with Malika.

"The whole thing started when my mother and I were standing on the terrace. And while we were out there we saw Malika standing across the street talking to some random lady. And in all of a sudden the lady hands Malika her cell phone. And right after she took the phone I saw her pressing the keypad. So that was a clear indication that she was calling somebody, right?"

"That's what people normally do when they dial a number."

"Exactly. So I rushed outside to confront her. But by the time I got out there she had already given the lady her phone back. So when I questioned her she stands there in my face and lies about having the lady's phone in the first place."

"You have got to be kidding me?" Damian interjected.

"No I'm not. But the kicker is, after she lied to me about having the cell phone in her possession, she had the audacity to go to my mother's apartment and change her story."

"What did she tell her?"

"She told my mother that she did use that lady's phone but she only used it to call her best friend. And that the only reason why she lied to me was because she knew I wouldn't believe her."

"When did she get a best friend?" Damian asked me.

"I asked her that very same question."

"And what did she say?"

"She got smart with me. And then she started cussing me out like her mind was going bad."

"And what was your mother doing while all of this was going on?"

"She kept telling us to stop arguing and let it go. But Malika kept running her mouth so I became the bigger person and left."

"Has she been over here since you left?"

"Who Malika?"

"Yeah."

"Nope."

"Well you know you're gonna have to tell Reggie what happened."

"Yes I know. But mom says that I shouldn't."

"Listen Naomi, I love your mother to death and I value her opinion. But in this case, you can't listen to her. Malika compromised our location and put us all at risk. And in my opinion everyone needs to know about it so that we can make some necessary decisions."

"But what if mother finds out? She's going to be mad with me."

"Would you rather for your mother to be angry? Or would you rather the Feds run up in here and arrest all of us?" Damian reasoned.

And I had to agree that getting arrested definitely out weighed my mother being mad with me because I blew Malika's spot up. "I'd rather have my mother be mad with me. I mean, she'll get over it faster than I'd be able to get out of jail."

"So then, it's settled. We're gonna have an emergency meeting." Damian told me.

"When will this meeting take place?"

"I'm gonna call Reggie now and see if he and Foxx can come here in the next few minutes."

"All right," I said. And laid my head back against the headboard of my bed.

I watched Damian while he called both Reggie and Foxx. Both of them agreed to meet at our place in the next fifteen minutes.

While we waited for Reggie and Foxx to arrive, Damian brought me up to speed about the meeting Reggie and Foxx had with the Mexican cats. "Did you sit in on the meeting?" I asked.

"No, but Foxx told me everything they agreed on."

"Well did you get a chance to see the guys?"

"Yeah, I saw them. And what I admired about them was that they weren't dressed like they were a part of a drug cartel. They wore regular button down shirts and blue jeans."

"What were they driving?"

"You ain't gonna believe it if I tell you."

"Try me."

"Those cats were driving in a 2002 Dodge pick-up truck. They could pass off as being construction workers any day of the week."

"That's a very smart move on their part."

"That's what I said."

"So, tell me how Foxx said the meeting with them went?"

"He said that they're gonna give us the coke for twenty-five a brick. But that amount is based under the condition that we cop at least four a week."

"I know Foxx didn't go for that."

"Oh yes, he did."

"I don't believe it."

"Well, believe it because it's true. And tonight we're meeting up with them to make the first trade."

"I don't understand why Foxx would agree to buy four kilos of coke from those guys when we haven't even set up shop yet. That's a serious dummy move he made." I commented.

"Well from what I was told on the drive back here, George is going to put Foxx and Reggie in touch with his nephew so he'll help us get rid of the product."

"Who's this nephew of George? And where does he come from? I mean we can't be linking up with random ass people just so we can make a quick buck. That ain't how we roll. We have always taken shit one-step at a time. So why do things any different?" I complained. I wasn't happy about anything Damian was telling me.

"Look, I'm just the messenger. When Foxx and Reggie get here, they'll be able to explain everything more in-depth."

"They're gonna have to do something because I'm not taking anymore risks. I'm gonna stay out here on these streets as long as I possibly can. And if I do end up getting picked up, it won't be because of someone else's negligence. I can guarantee you that much."

"Just calm down and let's see what happens." Damian insisted.

I did calm down but that mood quickly changed when Reggie and Foxx entered into my apartment.

Foxx was all over me. He kissed me and told me at least three times how much I was still his little girl and that he loved me since I was inside of my mother's womb. "Why you so happy?" I asked him.

"Because I've got my family here with me and everybody is all right." He explained.

"Tell her the other reason why you're happy." Reggie blurted out.

Damian, Foxx, Reggie and myself were sitting in the living room area of my apartment when Reggie insisted that Foxx tell me why he was really happy. I sat there and waited for Foxx to take the floor. And when he finally did, he said, "We're gonna be so rich that we'll be able to go into retirement in the next year."

"And how is that gonna happen?" I encouraged him to continue talking. I knew that he was talking about the drug deal he'd just made with the new guys from the Mexican cartel, but I wanted to hear it from his own mouth.

"Well, during the meeting with the Mexicans I arranged for us to get four kilos per week for twenty-five grand. And with those prices, we can get rid of three of them at market value for thirty-five and then we can break down the last one and sell it off piece by piece."

"Why four kilos? Who in the world would we be able to sell them to?"

"George is setting us up with his nephew and he's gonna handle everything for us." Foxx explained.

"Handle things, how? And have you even met this guy?" I pressed the issue. I wanted to know what was really going on in my father's head. I knew he used to run the streets back when I was a kid but the streets have changed since he last retired. So, it's not humanly possible to conduct business in this day and time like you did ten, fifteen years ago. It wouldn't work."

"Stop worrying so much. I've got everything under control." Foxx told me.

"I'm sure you do. But what if something goes wrong?" I pressed the issue. I needed him to be a little more up front with me. It wasn't just his ass on the line it was all of us.

"Nothing is going to go wrong. I have a solid plan in place with good people helping, so we're going to be fine."

Realizing that Foxx wasn't going to give me the information I needed, I turned to Reggie and asked him how he felt about it.

"I wasn't too happy about the deal in the beginning. But when he explained to me how we were going to get rid of it I was good."

"So he told you how things would work, but he's holding back on me?" I commented sarcastically. I was becoming more and more angrier by the minute. First it had to deal with Malika, now it was my own fucking family. What's next?

"Naomi, trust me, it's best this way sweetheart! The less you know, the better off you'll be." Foxx told me.

But I didn't agree with him. I knew the streets like the back of my hand. I made million-dollar deals for Reggie and myself. And I carried the load of our last operation like a soldier so how dare my father tell me that it was best that I didn't know what was going on? Had he lost his fucking mind?

"Everyone in this room knows that I can hold my own. I've hung with the best of them. And I've partnered with the some of the wealthiest men from around the world. So for you to act like I'm some type of amateur is a slap in the face."

"I understand why you're upset," Foxx interjected, " but sweetheart, we're only doing this for your good. Remember you were working for the airlines before the Feds shut you guys operation down. So it's more likely that your picture would show up on a local news station than your brothers."

"Yeah, Naomi, Foxx is right. We got to keep you behind the scenes so that no one recognizes you and blows the whistle on us." Reggie chimed in.

"I'm sorry, but it's probably too late for that." I blurted out.

Reggie and Foxx looked at me with a puzzled expression. "What do you mean, it might be too late?" Foxx inquired.

Yeah, what's up? Reggie asked.

"You'll find out soon enough." I commented.

We got a weak link amongst us.

CHAPTER FOURTEEN
Where Is The Loyalty?

Foxx and I were caught off guard after Naomi made the comment that our cover may have been blown. And not being willing to bring us up to speed about it, put me on edge. We wanted to know what was really going on. And Foxx and I weren't going to leave Naomi's apartment until she told us.

"Tell us what's going on?" Reggie said.

"Yeah, baby. Tell us what you know." Fox added.

"I saw Malika standing across the street from this building talking to a lady and then a few minutes later the lady handed Malika her cell phone. So when I confronted her and asked her who was she talking to she lied and told me that she didn't have the lady's phone at all. One thing led to the next, a few words were said and then I stormed off. Not even ten minutes later, mom knocks on my door and tells me to come to her apartment. So I followed her and when I got there Malika was waiting in the kitchen. And when I realized that mom had brought me there to settle things with Malika, I was against it at first because I felt like if she lied to me the first time she'll do it a second time."

"Did she?" Reggie interjected.

"That's not for me to say. But I will say that I know for a fact that she used that lady's cell phone. And by doing that she put us all in harms way."

"Who did she call?" Reggie wanted to know.

"She told mom she called her best friend. But I seriously think she called somebody in her family."

Foxx let out a loud sigh. "This is not good." He commented.

"It sure isn't. That's why I think we should be coming up with a Plan B."

Listening to my sister tell me that my girl could have breached our location gave me a sick feeling in my stomach. All I could think about was ripping her tongue from her mouth without causing any harm to my baby. I also thought about kicking that bitch out of my crib but that wouldn't do me any good because she'd be leaving with my baby. And she'd have plenty of opportunities to rat us out. That would be a devastating blow to me and my family.

Foxx looked at me and waited to hear my thoughts. "Whatcha' think we should do about this?" he asked me.

"Yeah, what's on your mind?" Damian asked.

"I'm thinking about a way I can kill Malika and get away with it." I finally said.

"Well, we can't put any energy to that right now. What we need to focus on is an exist strategy just in case she dropped the ball on us." Foxx stated.

"Yeah, we need to figure out our next destination." Naomi chimed in.

"We can go back to my brother's spot in Omaha, Nebraska." Damian suggested. "It's a nice area and no one will be able to find us there either."

"Yeah, Damian's right. When he and I were there we didn't have to worry about anything. Everyone there basically minded their own business." Naomi agreed.

"Have you ever had a conversation about where Naomi and Damian where while we were still in New York?" Foxx asked me.

"No, I've never sat around and talked to her about my family. All she knew was that they were gone and that was it." I told them.

"Well, she sure made a comment back at mom's place about how I fucked a lot of drug dealers so you and I could get good coke prices." Naomi blurted out. She looked very angry too.

"She did what?" I said. I needed Naomi to repeat what she said so I could be clear and precise about how I was going to deal with this situation. It was no secret that Malika did a lot of talking after I left. The problem I had with it was that she went against everything I stood for and there was no coming back from that.

"She made me look like a whore in front of mom by insinuating that I slept with every drug dealer in the world. And I couldn't figure out where in the hell she could've gotten that information from because we don't travel in the same circle. So the only person that was left was you. But then I said to myself that my brother wouldn't tell that bitch any of my business.

"And you're right, 'cause I ain't that type of nigga."

"So where do you think she got it from?" Naomi pressed issue.

"Baby girl, I wish I had the answer. But I don't. But I will find out, though."

"You ain't gotta do that. It's pointless. We've got better shit to think about."

"Yeah, you need to find out who she really talked to. And that way we can figure out our strategy from there." Foxx said.

"Do you think we should call the meeting off tonight?" Damian wanted to know.

"No, I don't think we should call it off. Let's just play it by ear. And that way Reggie can get back with us after he has had a chance to talk to Malika." Foxx replied.

"Yeah, I think that would be a good move." Damian agreed.

"Okay. Well it's settled. Let's meet back here in the next hour. And then we'll go from there." Foxx said.

After we all agreed to meet back at Naomi's place, I tried to prepare myself mentally before I stood face-to-face with this no good ass bitch. I swear, I had no idea what I was going to do to her. But I did know that if she said the wrong thing out of her mouth, I was going to make her feel a lot of fucking pain. I gave that bitch the world. And this was her way of repaying me? How grimey can one bitch be? First it was Vanessa. Now it was this bitch.

Tell me why I keep fucking with dumb ass bitches?

CHAPTER FIFTEEN
Damian v.s. My Family

D amian locked the front door after Reggie and Foxx left the apartment. And then he sat back down beside me on the sofa. He wrapped his arms around my neck and made me lay my head on his chest. By doing this, he made me feel like he was here with me for the purpose of protecting me. And in my crazy mind, that made all my family drama worth it. "Whatcha' thinks gonna happen when he approaches Malika?

"It can go either way. He could beat her to death or walk away from her altogether." I said.

"I hope he doesn't hit her because she is carrying his baby."

"I don't give a fuck what he does at this point."

"Come on baby, you don't mean that."

"Damian, you have no idea what she put me through while you guys were gone. After she embarrassed me in front of mom, I really wanted to kill her myself."

"Well, I'm glad you left when you did."

"She should've been glad too."

"She probably was." Damian commented. "But let's not talk about her anymore. Let's discuss when we're gonna leave this place. I think the faster we go the better off we'll be. No one would even recognize us while we're there. And my brother would welcome us back with open arms."

"As bad as I wanna go, I don't think I'm gonna be able to leave if my parents don't come with us."

"Well, there's a chance that they might not want to. And if that happens, then you're gonna be forced to make a choice between them and me."

I sighed. "I know."

"Are you ready for that?"

"Not really,"

"Well, all I gotta say is don't let me down."

I wanted to respond to Damian's last comment but my mouth wouldn't open. I loved this man with all of my heart, but my loyalty was to my family. So, how could I make him understand that? I knew my words would fall on deaf ears so I immediately changed the subject.

"Did you get anything to eat while you were out?" I asked him.

"No. Why you hungry?"

"Yeah, I am."

"Wanna order chinese?"

"Yes, let's do that."

May the food will take my mind off the drama.

I'm Forever NEW YORK'S FINEST

Chapter Sixteen
This Bitch is a Traitor

When I returned back to my apartment Malika's ass wasn't there. I hadn't been gone that long so she couldn't be anywhere but at my parent's spot. So, I went straight there. Something on the inside of me told me that she knew I had talked to Naomi about the bullshit stunt she pulled while I was gone, so she ran into hiding. But whether she knew it or not, my parents weren't going to stop me from smacking the shit out of her ass. She deserved a major beat down for her stupid ass behavior. "Where is Malika?" I asked my mother when she opened the door.

"She's out on the terrace talking to your father." She told me.

Without any hesitation I headed to the terrace where my mother told me Malika and Foxx were. I heard bits and pieces of their conversation. The words didn't become clear until I was within several feet of them. I heard Foxx making her aware of how severe her actions were when she used that strangers cell phone to call New York.

He was talking a little too nice for me. I changed the whole mood of the conversation when I stepped onto the balcony. My only mission was to find out who she had contact with. "Who did you talk to back in New York?" I roared. It felt like I was spitting venom from my mouth. That's how furious I was.

"I called my best friend." She answered quickly.

"What's your best friend's name?" my questions continued as I grinded my teeth.

"Her name is Tiffany."

"Who the fuck is Tiffany? And how come I've never heard about her before?"

"I've mentioned her to you a couple times before," she answered. She tried to give me the sincerest expression she had. But it didn't work with me. I knew the bitch was lying to me. And I hated being lied to. As a matter of fact, it irritated me to the point that I blacked out and before I even realized it, I had lunged back and threw a left blow to her face. I punched her across her right eye and she immediately collapsed on the floor of the balcony.

"Hold up Reggie, what are you doing?" Foxx yelled as he scrambled to pick Malika up from the floor.

"Fuck her! This bitch doesn't give a fuck about us. All she cares about is her stupid ass family. I told her she could call her moms on one of those throwaway phones I had. But no, she had to go behind my back and use some fucking stranger's phone. And what's even more fucked up, is that when I give her a chance to come clean with me about who she really called, she stood there and lied right in my face. I sacrificed too much to let her bring me down." I snapped.

While I was cursing Malika out, my mother ran out to the balcony to see what was going on. When she saw Foxx helping Malika to her feet she had a mouthful to say. "What is wrong with you Reggie?" she yelled. "You know I taught you to never hit a woman."

"Mom, stay out of this." I yelled.

"Son, your mother is right." Fox interjected.

"Do y'all realize how much trouble she has possibly caused?" I argued. I needed my parents to understand that this bitch doesn't give a damn about them. She was just like all the other bitches I used to fuck with. The only difference was that this ho was pregnant my baby.

My mother stood firm as she helped Foxx carry Malika back into the house. "It doesn't matter Reggie. She's a woman and she carrying your child."

Totally ignoring Foxx and my mother I followed them into the living room. I wasn't going to let up until Malika told me who she really talked to when she made that call to New York.

"Malika, stop lying to me and tell me who you talked to back in New York." I demanded.

Crying hysterically with her hand covering the eye I hit, she said, "I told you I called my best friend Tiffany."

"You're a fucking liar! You don't have a best friend named Tiffany." I screamed and then I lunged at her one more time. I couldn't hit her this time because Foxx blocked me.

"What's wrong with you son? Are you crazy?" Foxx asked.

"No she's crazy for fucking with my family." I replied sarcastically.

"I didn't do anything wrong." Malika cried out as she continued to shield her eye.

"Well since you didn't do anything wrong tell me what you and your best friend talked about?" I barked. I could feel the veins in my temple popping out through my skin.

Foxx grabbed me by the arm. "Come on Reggie we got to take a walk."

"Nah, Foxx I ain't leaving until she tells me the truth. And then I wanna know why the fuck she disrespected Naomi. Don't nobody disrespect my mother-fucking family. I don't give a fuck who it is."

"Just let it go son." Foxx warned me.

I resisted him a little bit but when he whispered in my ear and told me I'd better leave before someone in the next apartment hears all the commotion and calls the police, I allowed him to lead me out of the apartment.

We started talking out in the hallway but then we figured it would be best to take our conversation back to Naomi's apartment.

Naomi answered the door this time. "Why are y'all back so soon? I thought we weren't going to meet until an hour from now." She said.

I pushed my way past her and found myself a seat on her sofa. Foxx ended up bringing her and

Damian up to speed about the fight between Malika and I.

Naomi covered her mouth and said, "Oh my God! You really punched her in her eye?"

"Yeah I did." I responded nonchalantly.

"Did you hit her to the point that it turned black and blue?" Naomi continued her questions.

"Yeah it started turning colors before Foxx dragged me out of the apartment."

"Where is she now?" Damian wanted to know.

"She's at my place with my wife. I'm sure she's there putting some ice around her eye to keep the swelling down." Foxx explained.

"Do you think she may call the police?" Naomi asked me.

"If she knows like I know, she better not." I said out loud.

"So what happened? How did it come to the point where you had to punch her in her face?" Damian asked.

"Yeah, tell us what happened?" Naomi added.

"When I went home to confront her she wasn't there. So I figured she couldn't be anywhere but at mom and Foxx's crib so when I got there and saw that she was talking to Foxx on the balcony, I stepped to her and asked her who she called back in New York. And when she gave me that bullshit ass answer that she called her best friend Tiffany, I lost my cool and hit her in her fucking eye. Less than a second later, she fell down on the floor."

"She didn't fall on her stomach, did she?" Naomi asked.

"No, she fell back on her ass." I assured her.

"Did you help her get back up?" Naomi continued.

"Fuck no! And I wanted to hit the bitch again. But Foxx blocked me."

"Did you get a chance to question her about who told her I fucked a whole bunch of drug dealers?"

"Nah but I did ask her why she disrespected you, but since mom and Foxx were all over me they prevented me from making her talk."

"So what are you going to do about the phone call situation?" Naomi asked.

"What can I do? The dumb bitch won't come clean and tell me the truth."

"I think he should just leave it alone." Foxx suggested.

"I don't think leaving it alone is a good idea." Naomi chimed in. "I saw her facial expression when I first confronted her about the phone call and that alone made me believe that she called her mother. And if my suspicions are correct then it won't be long before the feds come looking for us."

"What if we're wrong?" Foxx spoke up.

"And what if we're not?" Naomi said.

"Look, all I'm saying is that we shouldn't get worked up for nothing. I may not know a lot about your girlfriend. But judging from the way you hit her I believe that if she called someone other than her best friend Tiffany, she would've told you by now." Foxx continued.

"Foxx, I know you mean well. But Malika doesn't have a best friend named Tiffany. I don't even remember her having a best friend at all." Naomi said.

"Me neither." I agreed. I'd been busting my brain trying to figure out if I remembered that name. But I kept coming up empty handed.

"So what are we going to do now?" Damian asked.

"I don't know what you guys are going to do. But I'm going back to my place and try to prevent Malika from calling the cops." Foxx said. "If any of y'all need me, you know where to find me." He said and then he left.

I sat there quietly as Foxx left Naomi's apartment, thinking about what was going to be my next move. While I was in deep thought, Naomi started telling me about all the weird feelings she was having.

"Reggie I'm not having a good feeling about what went down today. I mean, my gut is telling me that something is going to go down very soon. And if we don't take a few precautionary measures, then we're going to be in big trouble."

I sat there and listened to my sister as she warned me. But I let her words go through one ear and right out the other. I knew she loved me. And I knew she meant well. But I wanted to do shit my way. And running from the Feds wasn't on my list. I was tired of running. I just wanted to chill out and make some money. Regardless of what happened, I'm going to remain a soldier.

I didn't stay at Naomi's spot much longer after Foxx left. I headed to my apartment, so I could blow off some steam but I was side tracked by no one other than Mrs. Brandi. It was kind of odd that she'd catch me on the elevator once again. It almost seemed like the bitch was stalking me. "Where are you on your way to?" She asked me.

My mind was on the bullshit drama that happened earlier so the only answer I could give her was to tell her that I was going with her. She smiled and said, "Are you sure about that? I mean, you did act like you were afraid to open your mouth the last time I saw you and your girlfriend together."

"What was I supposed to do? I asked her. This bitch was tripping. She was acting like she wanted me to introduce her to Malika and carry on a conversation with her. Was she fucking crazy?

"Never mind about all of that. My husband's flight got delayed, so he's not coming in until tonight. So, why don't you join me at my place so we can go for round two." She smiled.

I was down for some more of her pussy. Especially since it was free and juicy. And the fact that we could get down and dirty at her spot made things very easy. My dick got hard just looking at her fat ass in those little ass shorts she wore. I saw the pink lining of her thong through her shorts too. This bitch was bad and she knew it too.

I moved up close behind her and started grinding on her ass. "Think I can get you to suck on my dick this time?" I asked her.

"I'll do anything for you." She replied seductively. This bitch was ready to drop her panties and I was all for it.

I followed her to her apartment after we got off the elevator. She had it smelling real good in there too. It smelled like she had over a dozen plugins all around her place. This definitely set the mood for me.

I didn't waste anytime with her. As soon as she locked the front door behind us, I stopped her in the foyer and started kissing on her neck while I continued to grind on her ass. My dick was rock hard at this point and I wanted to fuck her right there on the spot. But instead of sliding my dick inside of her, I turned her around and made her get down on her knees while I unzipped my pants. "You ready to suck on it?" I asked her.

She looked me in my eyes and said, "You know I am, so pull it out. I wanna make you feel real good."

There's nothing like getting head from a pro.

CHAPTER SEVENTEEN
A New Identity

With everything happening so fast, Damian thought it would be a good idea for he and I to go out to one of these department stores on the block to stock up on a few items. Our plan was to get a few things that would help create new identities for ourselves. Reggie and Foxx were taking this thing with Malika lightly. But Damian and I weren't. We felt it was important for us to have some disguises just in case we had to make an emergency getaway.

We walked into the local department store not far from the apartment. Damian and I both picked up several hats and ball caps. We also picked up a few clothing items. Nothing fancy, just a few pieces of attire to make us look older than we were. After we left the department store we found a wig shop owned by a Korean family. Those fucking Asians were happy to see us, especially since we dropped a few hundred bucks on several wigs and make-up. And once we were done there, we decided to take a drive so that we could talk further.

"Naomi you know there's a strong possibility that your family isn't gonna want to leave this place."

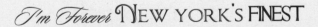

Damian pointed out.

I let out a loud sigh and said, "Yes, I know."

"So what are you going to do?" Damian pressed the issue. I could tell that he wasn't going to let me off the hook.

"Well I'm gonna talk to mama first and then I'll be able to make my decision from there." I told him.

"What if she says she's not gonna leave without Foxx?"

"Then I guess I'm gonna have to figure out a way to move on without her." I lied. I couldn't tell him my true feelings because he wouldn't understand. My family was my life. And I was always taught to never put anyone before them. Our love for one another was strong and unbreakable. So, that was the burden that I carried.

"I really hope you mean that." He commented as he looked at me and then he put his attention back on the road ahead of us.

"I do." I lied once more.

"Good. Because I've been talking to my brother Champ and he said that his doors are always open. Not only that, he told me he had a job for us when we decide to go back. That way we won't spend all of our stash money."

"A job doing what?"

"He and his wife just started a medical transportation business. And he said that they needed a lot of help with running the office part." Damian explained.

"Oh okay." I said, but I wasn't really pressed about it. I honestly couldn't think that far ahead. I was more concerned with the present. Anything outside of that was a non-motherfucking factor.

"Let me ask you another question?" Damian said.

"Sure go ahead."

"I know we've never talked about this before so I'm gonna ask you how you feel about having kids?"

I had to admit that I was truly caught off guard by Damian's question. Children were precious to me. And I would love to have some one-day but today was just not the day. I mean how could he talk about children when we were trapped in this big mess? I understood that he may be dealing with some issues concerning having a family of his own but now wasn't a good time to talk about it.

Instead of giving him the cold shoulder and brushing him off, I used kid gloves to let him down easy.

"I would love to have kids. But you know with everything that's going on right now, I would hate to bring a child into this world not knowing whether we are going to be here to raise 'em. I mean, anything could happen. You could get locked up. I could get locked up. And then what would happen to our baby if either one of those things happen?"

"My family could jump in and take over that situation at any moment. Your parents could do it too." He suggested.

"You're right. But that wouldn't be fair to our baby. So I'll say this, once all of this mess is behind us then we can entertain the idea."

"Okay. That's fair." He agreed. "But don't get amnesia when I bring the subject back up at a later date.

I gave him a half smile. "I won't." I assured him.

I gotta admit that Damian is a good man.

CHAPTER EIGHTEEN
The Voice of Reason

I didn't run off on Brandi this time around. She did a brother right once again so I spent about an hour with her. I fucked around and almost told her that my real name was Reggie after she called me Jimmy a couple times. Besides that hiccup, we chilled out and talked about how long she and her husband been together and how they rarely ever spent time together. I started feeling sorry for her after she told me she'd only see him like five days in an entire month.

"Have you ever fucked around on him before me?"

"When you put it that way it sounds really harsh."

"I'm sorry. But it is what it is."

"Well, to be honest, I've never screwed around on him until I met you." She said. But I knew she was lying.

Jump-offs like her always kept a nigga on the side. And as much as her husband was on the road, there was no question in my mind that he fucked around on her to.

"Since you ain't never fucked around on him tell me why you got with me?" I asked. I was curious to hear her answer. I was always open to a little bit of comic relief every so often. Not only that, I loved when bitches like her, blew smoke up my ass.

She tried to give me the most seductive smile she had. And I had to admit that it worked for a minute or two.

"I got with you because you had that certain spark that I hadn't been getting from my husband."

"And what kind of spark is that?"

She smiled once again. "You just had this certain swag about yourself. You're sexy. You're confident. And you know how to take control of a situation."

I smiled. "Yeah, that's about right."

"Can I ask you a question?"

"Yeah go-ahead."

"How far along is your girlfriend?"

"She's due any day now."

"Is that your first baby?"

"Yep."

"Is it a girl or a boy?"

"Didn't you say you wanted to ask me a question?"

"Yes."

"And a question means one, right?"

"Yes."

"A'ight, well no more questions about my girl and my baby."

"Sorry. My bad! I won't ask you any more questions about her."

"Thank you."

"So when can I see you again?"

"Isn't your husband coming home later?"

"Yes,"

"So, how can I make that call when he's gonna be here?"

"He's not gonna be in town long. Trust me, he'll be out of here in the next couple of days. If not tomorrow."

"Well, just hit me up after he leaves,"

"How can I do that when I don't have your number?"

I kissed her on her forchcad and then I said, "Send me a smoke signal. Immediately after I kissed her I told her I had fun and that it was time for me to go. She walked me to the door looking like a sad puppy dog.

←—————————————————————————→

I hopped in the shower as soon as I got back to my apartment. I had to wash that pussy smell off my dick before Malika smelled it. Speaking of Malika, I thought the bitch would be here by now but I guessed she wasn't ready to come back home. I wasn't going to sweat it. I figured she got what she deserved and that was about the end of it.

While I was dressing I heard my front door open. I knew it was Malika so I left the bedroom to greet her. I was surprised to see that it was my mother. "Whatcha' doing here?" I asked her.

"Is that anyway to greet your mother?"

"I didn't mean it like that. I'm just shocked to see you here, that's all."

"I came to get Malika a change of clothes since she's not ready to come back home yet."

"I don't care what she wants because she's coming back here tonight whether she likes it or not."

"Son you can't treat her like that. She's a woman. And she's the mother of your unborn child. How would you feel if another man smacked and punched your daughter around? You wouldn't like that very much, would you?"

"Of course not. It wouldn't happen. I would kill a man if he put his hands on my daughter."

"So, you admit that you were wrong for putting your hands on her?" My mother pressed the issue.

"Yeah, I know I was wrong. But I feel like when someone is trying to hurt my family, all bets are off. I would kill for my family. So when she did what she did, I kind of lost my cool."

"You did more than that." My mother rolled her eyes.

"See mom, you just don't understand."

"Oh, I understand more than you know. That's why I've been in Malika's ear all afternoon trying to keep her from calling the police."

"Oh, so now she wants to call the cops on me? She knows I don't play that calling the police shit!"

"You better watch your mouth around me." My mother snapped.

"I'm sorry mom. I just got so much stuff on my mind."

"I know you got a lot of stuff on your mind. But you have to be mindful that you're not the only one going through changes. That girl is lying in my guest bedroom crying her heart out because she's hurt and she feels like she's alone.

"Why in the world does she think she's alone? She got me. She got you and Foxx."

"Having us is not the same as having her family. She feels like you are cheating her out of time that she can spend with her family."

"Mom, she knows the situation. She knows I can't pack up and go back to New York with her. So why even talk about it?"

"Reggie you've got to realize that she's a woman and she has feelings. Women don't operate the same way men do. So things that matter to us may not matter to you. And I'm saying all of this because you're gonna have to come to a compromise with her concerning her family."

"I'm sorry mom. But I can't do that."

"And why not?"

"If I let her go back to New York I feel like I may not ever see my baby anymore. And I can't take that chance."

"Well what would you do if she left one day while you're with your father?"

"I'll be pissed off. And if I'm mad enough I may even go looking for her."

I'm Forever NEW YORK'S FINEST

"And that's why you need to be more considerate of her feelings."

"But, mom...."

"But mom nothing. Give her a chance so this whole thing doesn't backfire on you."

"Since y'all were doing a whole bunch of talking, did she tell you what her and her best friend Tiffany were talking about?"

"She told me we should make a phone call, Tiffany didn't answer. So she left her a message and told her that she'll call back when she got a chance."

"And you believed that?"

"Listen son, I give people a little bit of rope at a time. Now if what she told me was a lie, then she'll eventually hang herself."

I smiled at my mother because she was a very smart woman. Now I see why Foxx stuck in there with her all these years. "Mom, how did you become such a wise woman?"

"When I was young I used to sit around while my father and my uncles used to congregate in the basement of our house and play dominoes. I would sit there and listen to all their stories about the women they were married to. And after listening to it for so long I knew what it took to keep your father happy even when he and I first started dating. So, you see, being in a relationship isn't hard. People make it hard when they're not willing to give up anything."

I smiled at my mother once again. And then I leaned over and hugged her. "You're the best! You know that."

"Of course, I do." She said.

"Well, before you go can you do me a favor?"

"Sure. What is it son?"

"Can you please make sure that Malika doesn't use any of the phones in your apartment? I would hate for her to bring the Feds right to our front door."

"Don't worry. I'll keep my eyes on her. But you better do your part by her as well," she urged me.

"I will." I replied and then I smiled.

Happy wife....happy life!

CHAPTER NINETEEN
Waiting for the Call

"**O**kay. I'll be ready when you get here." Damian said and then he disconnected the call.

I knew it was Foxx calling before Damian ended the call. I just had that vibe from this conversation.

"So, you guys are getting ready to leave, huh?" I asked. I was in the kitchen throwing away the container that I ate my Chinese food from.

"Yeah. Foxx said he just got a call from George and that we'll be leaving in a few minutes."

"How do you feel about it?"

"You mean the meeting?"

"Yeah."

"Well it ain't like this is my first time picking up a load of product. That part is easy. So, I'm cool. But picking up four bricks and trusting a nigga we don't even know to get rid of it for us is the dumbest decision a man could make. I'm not feeling that shit at all."

"Did you ever get a chance to talk to Foxx about it?"

"Nah. I'm just gonna leave it alone. I told you I'm gonna play the backseat this time around."

"Well, if that's what you want to do, then I'm fine

with it." I said and then I changed the subject. "I've been thinking about Malika since Reggie left and I can't believe I'm starting to feel sorry for her ass!"

"That's because you have a good heart."

"Damian, I'm trying to be serious now."

"Me too."

I sighed heavily. "I just wished that none of this shit ever happened. And I'm talking about everything." I began to explain. "I believe that if I would've just done my job at the airlines we wouldn't be in shit situation. I'd still be working and we'd all still be living in New York."

"Now I know you're not blaming yourself for everything that happened?"

"Let's face it Damian, all of this mess started from my fucked up ass connections. If I wouldn't have set Reggie up with Miguel and Marco none of this shit would've happened."

Damian grabbed me into his arms. My butt was against the countertop. "'I'm not going to stand here and let you take blame for this. Even if you had never arranged for Marco and Reggie to do business together, who's to say that this situation would not have happened with anyone else? When you're in the game, shit like this happens. And unfortunately it happens to everyone. You either get picked up by the Feds or your family buries you. Take your pick. No one escapes. And that's the bottom line. So stop acting like you brought this on us because you didn't."

"I understand everything you're saying, but I'm

still feeling a little guilty inside."

"Well let it go! You're beating yourself up for nothing. Right now all you need to focus on is making sure your family is fine and everything else will fall into place."

"If you say so," I commented. I really wanted him to drop the conversation. It didn't matter what he said to me because I still felt like my family was in this mess because of me. And that's the main reason why it would be hard for me to leave them behind. Whether Damian wanted to believe it or not, I wasn't just dealing with the issue of leaving my family, I felt responsible for them. So, in the end he's going to have to realize that my family is a package deal. There was nothing but hell that would separate me from them. And if he wanted to keep this relationship with me alive, then he's going to have to make some sacrifices. Marrying me means he would also have to marry my family. If someone had to die between my father and him, he'd have to take the bullet because my loyalty was to Foxx. I can't speak for Damian and his family, but I knew how things worked with my people. If you didn't conform to the ways of my family then you had to go. That's it. And I can't put it any simpler than that. It is what it is.

Foxx and Reggie finally made their way to the apartment to get Damian. Before they left, I told them to be careful. But most importantly, I told them to keep their phones on and to call me if anything went wrong.

Foxx and Reggie blew me off as if to say they wouldn't need my help. That was just a man thing with those two. They've always been like that. But Damian on the other hand, promised me that he'd call me if the deal went sour. I appreciated it too.

Gotta' hold my three men down!

CHAPTER TWENTY
The Trade-off

I n route to George's sub shop Foxx went over the plan with me again. "Reggie, I want you to hold onto the money until I check out the product. After I test all four bricks and everything looks good I'll give you the queue to hand over the money. So once you take the money out I want you to stuff the same bag with the product."

"Think we ought to let them see our hardware?" I asked.

"No. They don't need to see our guns. Let's keep them under wraps."

"Did George tell you how many were supposed to be there?"

"He didn't say. But I'm sure Ernesto and Angel will be the ones to make the actual trade." Foxx told me.

"Do you still want me to stay in the car?" Damian asked Foxx.

"Yeah. We need you covering our ass from the outside. That way we don't have to worry about any unexpected visitors."

After Foxx gave precise instructions, we all set back in the car and talked about the situation with Malika and I. Foxx wouldn't let me off the hook about the fact I gave Malika a black eye. I knew I was wrong but in my mind she somewhat deserved what she got.

"Have you seen her eye since the fight?" Foxx asked me.

"Nah. Haven't seen her." I told him.

"Your mother told me she spoke with you concerning the situation with Malika." Foxx continued.

"Yeah, she said her peace."

"How did you feel about what she said?"

"Foxx I'll put it to you like this, mom doesn't know everything that Malika and I have been through. So she'll never understand the way I handle things. All she knows is that she saw me hit Malika. That's it. So, if I tried to justify my actions concerning Malika she isn't going to agree with it. So, I just let the chips fall where they may."

"Did she tell you she stopped Malika from calling the police?"

"Yeah. She told me."

"And how did you feel about that?"

"Did she do it?"

"No."

"Well, I don't have any feelings about it."

"Do you believe she talked to someone when she made that phone call?" Foxx questions continued.

"Of course I do. And I don't believe it was a chick named Tiffany either. She blew smoke up mom's ass and mom went for it."

"I believe she talk to someone too." Damian

spoke up. "And from the looks of it, she's gonna stick to her guns and ride that lie until the wheels fall off."

"I know she is. But, I'm gonna come out on top in the end." I commented. It seemed like the more I talked about Malika, the angrier I got. My gut feeling was telling me that Malika wasn't telling us everything. That bitch was hiding more than just who she talked to on the phone. She had more skeletons in her closet and it won't be long before they were revealed to me. I wasn't the smartest nigga in the world, but I had common sense and that was all I needed.

Damian pulled up in the parking lot of George's sub shop. George had given us instructions to park our vehicle in the back of the shop so we wouldn't draw any attention to his shop since it was already closed.

From the looks of it, George's car was the only one here so that meant that our Mexican connection hadn't made it yet.

"Think we outta' go inside?" I asked Foxx.

"Yes of course." Foxx replied.

After Damian put the car in park, Foxx and I got out and knocked on the back door. George let us in and led us into h   office that was tucked away in the back of his sub sh .

He had a sm l sofa next to his desk so Foxx and I grabbed us a seat. I kept the money tucked away underneath my arm until it was time for me to make the trade-off.

"Spoke with your guys?" Foxx asked George.

"Yeah, they should be here any minute now," he

said.

"Have you spoken to your nephew since the last time we spoke?" Foxx continued to question George.

"Yeah, I spoke with him tonight. And he's all set and ready to go to work."

Five minutes into a conversation about George's nephew we heard a knock on the back door. Immediately after he opened the door and let Ernesto and Angel inside we all got in a huddle and handled business as usual.

Without any hesitation, Angel pulled all four kilos of cocaine from his duffle bag. Ernesto tore a small hole in the bag with a pocketknife and dug the tip of it inside the coke. "Try it my friend," he said to Foxx.

But Foxx wasn't interested in testing the purity of the coke. So I stepped up to the plate and took the liberty to do it myself. After I sniffed the dope up my nose I damn near went into cardiac arrest. My nose couldn't take the purity of the product. I literally started choking and everything. George had to hand me a napkin from his desk.

"Are you all right my friend?" Angel asked.

I used the napkin George handed me and tried to blow out every morsel of coke I had attached to the membranes in my nose. "All I gotta say is that your product is some potent shit."

Both men smiled. "That's what we like to hear." Angel said.

"I see the fish scales in here to." I said as I inspected all three kilos.

"We sell nothing but the best." Ernesto said.

"If you guys keep the product just like this, you'll have us as customers as long as we're in the game."

"Yes, that's what we like to hear." Ernesto commented.

"So, do you have our money?" Angel asked as he looked at both of us.

Foxx gave me the signal to hand him the money-bag. Immediately after I had given him the bag containing one hundred grand, he handed it to Angel. Angel then handed it to Ernesto. Ernesto looked inside the bag and then he closed it up. "It's all here," he said to Angel.

Angel smiled at Foxx. "Well, I guess this concludes our meeting."

I guess it does." Foxx replied.

Everyone stood up from their seats, including George. Like always George would excuse himself to walk Ernesto and Angel to the door. This was a common choice of action when someone is leaving your domain.

After he let them out he returned to his office and stood next to his desk. "So, are you cool with the product?" he wondered aloud.

"Yes, everything looks good." Foxx told him.

"Well, let's get on out of here so we can head on to my nephew's place."

"I'm ready as ever." Foxx said.

"Roger that," I said.

←—————————————————————————————→

Foxx decided to ride with George in route to George's nephew house. George told us we were going to a neighborhood called Ivy Wild here in Denver. But we still had no idea how to get there. So Damian and I followed behind them. The drugs rode in the car with Damian and I.

They were tucked away in the bag by my feet on the car floor. "How does the coke look?" Damian wanted to know.

"All four kilos look really good. And when I tasted it the shit almost got me sick."

"Oh, well that sounds like some potent shit."

"Yeah, it is."

"How do you feel about those Mexican cats?"

"I ain't trying to be their best friends. But they seem all right. Why you ask that?"

"When I saw them walk out the shop, they started talking and laughing and shit. And I just wasn't feeling their vibe."

"Well, I don't know what they were laughing about because everything was on the up and up while we were making the trade. So whatever they had going on doesn't concern us. I figured as long as we are straight on this end, fuck 'em."

"Did George tell you how far we had to drive?

"Yeah. He said we were about ten minutes away

from his nephew's spot. And I heard him saying something about we might pass a couple of cops so we might be going to the hood."

"As long as we don't run into niggas trying to rob us or get pulled over, I'm cool."

I cracked a smile. "I feel you." I told Damian. He was right. We didn't need any unnecessary interference. All we wanted to do was pick up the dope and drop it off after we cut it up a little bit. That's it. We weren't asking for anything more than that.

Ivy Wild was just like I had pictured it. An area filled with low-income housing, drug addicts and junkies walking in the streets and prostitutes trying to score their next blowjob so they can come up on a few dollars. Fortunately we didn't pass any cops. But we got our fair share of niggas running up to our cars to see if they could get us to score some of their dope. "You got the wrong car." I yelled through the window.

Once we got through the small crowd Damian and I followed George and Foxx to Dorchester Drive. After we parked our cars I gave Damian instructions to stay in the car with the product while I go with Foxx to meet George's nephew.

Damian locked the car door and left the car running while Foxx and I checked things out. I couldn't tell you why my heart was racing like it was because I wasn't afraid of anything. So, I figured maybe I was dealing with some sort of anxiety issues. But whatever it was it wasn't normal for me.

We followed George to this two-story house. It

looked old and rundown. There were at least five broke down vehicles on the land surrounding the house. Not too far from the house was a trailer park. Those trailer park houses were also rundown. I smelled white trash instantly.

"Does anybody live here?" I asked George.

"No. But this is a stash house. My nephew runs it."

"Do you think its safe for us to go in there?"

"Yeah. We're good as long as we don't stand here long." He warned us.

As we approached the house the door slowly opened. Not too long after a head appears around the door. I couldn't get a clear visual of the guy because of how dark it was outside but I knew he was a nigga after he said, "Unc is those your people?"

When I tell you this nigga was country as hell. Believe me. And I assumed Unc was short for uncle. But from the looks of it, this nigga looked nothing like George. Maybe George was a distant uncle or something. It really didn't matter either way. I was more concerned about the business part of this meeting so I didn't say a word while they sorted through the preliminaries. I knew how to stand in my own lane and that's what Foxx and I did.

"Yeah, these are the guys I was telling you about." George replied.

"Are they packing?"

"Yeah they are. But they're good. You aren't gonna have any problems."

The nephew thought for a second and then he said, "A'ight." And then the door opened wider so we could go inside.

I looked back at Damian once more before I stepped cross the threshold. Damian was sitting up in the front seat and he seemed like he was alert so I figured he was good and allowed the cat behind the door to close it.

The inside of the house was dark at first, so I kept my hands on my pistol at all times.

"Why is it so dark in here?" I spoke up. This cat had us walking down a dark hallway. I wasn't feeling this shit at all.

"Oh don't worry. My nephew keeps the front of the house dark to create the illusion that no one is here. If you would've noticed when you first walked in the door that he had wool blankets covering the front windows." George explained.

"Nah, it was too dark. I couldn't see anything." I replied.

"Well we'll have some light as soon as we get on the other side of that door." His nephew pointed out. And just like he had mentioned, light was definitely on the other side of the door. We entered into the den and kitchen area of the house. The lights in this part of the house were bright as hell. It damn neared blinded me.

Foxx and I stood by the door after George's nephew closed it. George stood next to us and began to introduce all parties involved. There were three guys total in the room. George's nephew was standing a couple of feet away from George. He was a short, thin guy. He had to be every bit of 5'5. He was dark as hell too. But he had some white ass teeth. He looked like he was of African descent. But it was clear that he wasn't. George introduced him as Keith. The other two guys looked the exact opposite. They were both light brown skin. They resembled one another so I assumed they were brothers. From what I could tell they were a few inches taller than Keith. George introduced them both to us as well. "Foxx and Reggie these two guys are Keith's friends, C.W. and his brother Mikey."

"What's up?" I said. Foxx gave them a nod. And both cats nodded back.

"So, what's the plan?" Keith asked.

I looked at George and gave him the green light to answer his nephew's question. I would've been out of pocket if I would've spoke up. I was on someone else's territory so I had to have someone vouch for me and since George was the cat who co-signed for us, we had to let him break the ice. "Foxx and Reggie want you guys to get rid of their coke in exchange for a share of the profits." George explained.

"How much is in it for us?" Keith wanted to know.

George looked at Foxx and then he looked at me. It was apparent to me that Foxx didn't know what to say so I spoke up. "How much traffic you got coming through here?" I asked Keith.

"Why you wanna know that for?" Keith stood his

ground.

"I need to know how much we can trust you with in one delivery. That way we can calculate the numbers and give you a specific number." I stated.

"If you give us two keys we could get rid of them in three days tops." Keith said.

I looked at George and then I looked at Foxx. I needed for someone to co-sign what this cat was saying. I swear I couldn't see this nigga getting rid of two bricks in less than three days. Yeah, he had traffic outside his spot but it wasn't enough to put a dent in a half of kilo.

When George or Foxx didn't say anything I had to put George on the chopping block. He knew more about his fucking nephew than me. So, I needed him to help shed light on this matter. "George, is it true that he can get rid of two bricks in a couple days?"

"Yeah, if it's around payday, he can make it happen." George answered.

"What's your specialty?" I asked.

"We normally do eight balls, quarter ounces, half ounces and ounces. But if we get somebody looking for four and a half or a quarter key and we got it, we'll sell it to 'em."

"Do you sell it in rock or powder?"

"Both. If you give me half rock and half powder, that'll be good."

"How would you feel if we bag the coke up for you?"

"I'd prefer you give it to us and let us do it because we know how much to give our customers. But if you wanna bag it up yourself then that's cool too."

"Whatcha' think Foxx? Wanna drop two of 'em on him or one?" I asked.

The room became silent, awaiting Foxx's answer. "Let's start him off with one of them and then when he's done with that, we can come back and hit him off with the other one." Foxx answered.

"A'ight, well there it is. We're gonna hit you off with one and after you've did your thing with that, call us and we'll come back and give you the other one." I reiterated to Keith.

"Okay, cool." Keith said.

"A'ight people well since we got that straightened out, we'll get back with you in a couple of hours." I told him.

"So, you ain't got the shit now?" Keith asked.

"Nah, we don't have it. But don't worry we'll have it back here in the next few hours." I assured them.

Keith looked at George like he was surprised by my answer or thrown off by my response concerning the coke. It became very clear that Keith and his boys were under the assumption that we were going to be dropping off the coke now. Was he crazy? Foxx and I weren't giving these cats our product without cutting it up. We had to make some money off of it too.

Before we made our exit we gave them our word that we'd be back in a couple of hours after we took care of a few things. We also gave them our word that we'd give them the product in powder form. Keith and his boys acted like they were fine with our arrangement so we shook on it.

When we got back to the cars, Foxx said a few words to George and then he hopped in the car with Damian and I. I got back into the front seat while Foxx sat in the back. We followed George back out of the neighborhood and when we got back into the area of Denver that we were familiar with, George waved us off.

"Are you calling him back after we separate the coke?" I asked him.

"Yes, I think he should accompany us to that place at least until we become familiar with the area." Foxx replied.

"Did you see how Keith looked at George when we told him that we'll have to bring the coke back to the spot?" I asked Foxx. I needed to see if Foxx and I were on the same page.

"Yes, I saw it. But it was probably just them miscommunicating. It was no big deal." Foxx said.

"It may have been some miscommunicating going on but the way shit went down in there, I would bet money that George told him that we were meeting with the Mexicans tonight and that as soon as we got the merchandise that we were going to drop it off to them." I explained.

"George may have told them that we were on our way with the product but I don't think he'd go as far as telling them we made the trade tonight." Foxx replied.

"Well, I do."

"Well you're entitled to think whatever you want. But keep in mind that George is a very good friend of mine and he wouldn't fuck us over."

"Okay Foxx. You know him better than I do. So, I play behind the scenes and let you handle everything."

Good friend or not. I know the streets!

CHAPTER TWENTY-ONE

Four Days Later

My mother and I walked to the local supermarket and picked up a few things for dinner. We tried to get Malika to tag along with us but she refused to leave the apartment. For the past four days she's been staying in my parents guest room. Reggie tried to get her to come back to the apartment but she wouldn't budge. So, Reggie left her alone and started entertaining the jump-off chick Brandi on a regular basis. Reggie mentioned that Brandi's husband left town once again so he's been filling in while he's been away. There was no question in my mind that that man wouldn't hesitate killing his fucking wife if he knew that Reggie was fucking her on the nights he's been on the road. Talk about drama!

Upon entering back into the apartment my mother and I caught Malika in the kitchen pouring herself a glass of orange juice. My mother spoke to her first. "It's good to see you out of the room."

"I only came out to get a glass of juice." She replied.

My mother placed her bag of groceries on the table. "How are you feeling?"

Malika took a sip of her orange juice. "I still feel the same. I'm either cramping one minute and the next I'm feeling contractions in my lower back." She said after she swallowed the juice.

While my mother got Malika to do some small talk I watched her from the other side of the kitchen. I zoomed in on her eye and it looked pretty bad. This was my first time seeing her since the incident between her and Reggie happened. I'm glad I didn't see her eye when he'd first hit her because if it looked any worse than what it looked like now then she looked fucked up. There was definitely an elephant in the room. And the only way I'd be able to face this thing head on is if I addressed the issue she and I had that led to Reggie hitting her.

Right after my mother ended their conversation, Malika made a beeline for the bedroom she was occupying. But I stopped her right in her tracks. "Hey Malika, can I please talk to you for a minute?" I asked as I followed her to the entryway of the kitchen.

She tried to ignore me. But I was persistent. So I finally got her to turn around and face me in the hallway. We were exactly thirty feet away from the guest bedroom. She sighed heavily like I had a nerve stopping her in the first place. "What is it?" she asked abruptly.

Okay I got it. She was still upset with me about the cell phone incident. And I'm more than sure she blamed me for Reggie hitting her. So, knowing all of this, I felt the need to apologize to her even though I felt she lied. The discoloration around her eye made me feel sorry for her. I mean she looked fucking awful. "Look Malika, I know you may not want to hear this but I gotta tell you how sorry I am for all the shit that went down between you and my brother."

"Oh so now you're sorry?" she snapped. "You see my eye and now you want to apologize to me? Girl, keep your fucking apologies. Cause it's a little to late for that bullshit!"

"Damn, so it's like that?" I snapped back.

"Yeah, it's all the way like that."

I chuckled, looking at her from head to toe. "Here I was feeling sorry for your dumbass and this is the thanks I get? How ungrateful can you be?"

"I don't need you to feel sorry for me. You did enough by spreading lies to your brother."

"Wait a minute Malika, you're acting like I told Reggie to hit your ass! I spat. This bitch was taking this shit to another level and I wasn't having it.

"Why don't you just go fuck off!" She replied sarcastically and then she turned and stormed off to the bedroom. I started to curse her stupid ass out. But then I decided against it. I had better shit to do than run down behind that low budget bitch. What she needed to worry about was how she was going to convince Reggie to give her a pass so she could let her family see her baby because right now it isn't looking too good for the bitch.

My mother called my name so I assumed she needed me back in the kitchen and when I returned she had this disappointed expression on her face. "Mom, you want me?" I asked her.

"Yes.

"What's up?"

"Why do you have to constantly badger her?

Mom, are kidding me right now?

Of course I'm not. Why can't you just leave her alone?

I went back there to apologize to her. And instead of humbling herself she got all crazy with me.

Well, why don't you give her time to come to you?

Look I was just trying to clear the air so everybody could get along and go back to how things used to be.

And I appreciate that. But again, if you see that she is resisting you then leave it alone.

Okay. I'll do just that. I mean because I could care less either way. I was just trying to reach out to her for the sake of you and Reggie.

And I could care less my damn self! Malika blurted out. She literally came out of nowhere. I thought she went into my parents' guest room but instead, she was hiding behind the corner eavesdropping on my mother and I conversation.

My mother and I both turned around towards Malika. She was standing there with her hand draped over her shoulder like she was on her way out the door.

I stood there speechless, not knowing whether to tell her to go to hell or just let her have the floor so she could say whatever she wanted to. I was truly done with her altogether.

Malika, are you getting ready to go somewhere?

Yeah, I gotta' get out of here.

So where are you going?

Going to take a walk.

By yourself? My mother's questions continued.

Yeah.

Are you sure you want to do that. Because I could go with you if you like. My mother suggested.

No I'm fine. I won't be gone long. She replied and then she walked out the door.

My mother stood there in sheer panic mode. Do you think we should follow her? She asked me.

Somebody should. Because I've got a gut feeling that she's gonna make another call to New York.

Oh my God. We can't let that happen. Think we should call Reggie?

No. I'll handle it. I said and then I left out of the apartment immediately after Malika.

Malika had already gotten on the elevator by the time I left the apartment. So I raced to see what floor she was going to. I stood there and watched the numbers light up as the elevators passed each floor. And when I realized that she stopped on the first floor I raced down the staircase.

I was huffing and puffing like I was out of breath. I couldn't believe how unfit I was after running down seven flights of stairs. I made it down to the first floor in a matter of fifteen seconds. But when I scanned the lobby area I didn't see Malika insight. I raced to the revolving glass doors and once again she was not in sight. So, I raced over to the front desk and got the white man's attention standing behind it. "Excuse me, but did you see a pregnant black woman get off the elevator? And if so, did you see where she went?"

"No, I'm afraid not."

I sighed. "Well did you see anyone get off the elevator a few minutes ago?"

"No, I'm afraid I didn't. I was taking a call a few minutes ago so I can't say who walked where." He explained.

I looked at this fool like he was out of his damn mind. What in the hell was he here for? He was definitely not doing his job because if he was then he'd be monitoring that elevator better than he had. I really didn't have any more words for him. So, I just shook my head and walked away.

I figured she could not have gone anywhere else but outside so I exited the lobby with hopes of seeing her somewhere nearby. When I reached the curb directly outside of the apartment building I looked both ways once again nowhere in sight. "Where in the world is this dumb bitch at?" I mumbled. "She couldn't have gone that far. I was right behind her." I continued to mumble.

"Are you looking for something?" I heard a male voice ask me.

I turned around and it was the doorman dressed in his burgundy uniform and hat. He was a black guy and he was pretty old but his eyes looked like they worked fine. "Did you see a pregnant black woman leave this building a few minutes ago?" I asked him.

"Yes, as a matter of fact I did. She walked up the block like she was going towards the bus stop." He pointed out as he directed my attention towards the east.

When I looked in the direction the doorman was pointing I saw a ton of stores, which meant she could be in anyone of those places. And if I was going to find her then I needed to be very careful that I didn't run into her and blow my cover.

"Thank you very much." I said to the doorman and then I walked off in search of my brother's baby mama.

Chapter Twenty-Two
Brandi v.s. Malika

Since everything had been running smooth between George's nephew Keith and Foxx and I, I told him and Damian to go and pick up the last bit of dough Keith owed us so we could do our re-up run later on tonight. This time we were going to score twenty bricks. We got word from George that our Mexican connection was running out of product and that they were leaving to go re-up and that they will be gone for about four weeks if not more. This was their usual thing and how they ran their organization so that was why we opted to purchase what they had left so that we wouldn't run out.

While they were handling our business affairs I was at Brandi's apartment. Naomi knew I hadn't gone with Foxx and Damian but my mother thought otherwise. I had to let Naomi know where I was just in case she needed me for something. I also decided to stay behind because two weeks had passed and Malika still hadn't gone into labor. My mother assured me that everything seemed fine with Malika and that if she hadn't gone into labor in the next couple of days then she was going to take her to the hospital herself. I swear there was nothing like family.

Spending time with Brandi took my mind off the bullshit drama Malika and I was going through. I loved chilling with Brandi because she wasn't stingy with the pussy. And it was easy to talk to her even though most of the shit I told her was a lie. Not only that, I loved looking at how sexy she was too. Her body was banging and she was pretty too. She had the whole package deal. What else could a nigga ask for?

I was sitting on her living room sofa while she sat next to me. She had just gotten out of the shower so she was naked from head to toe. I reached over and started rubbing on her pussy so I could get it wet. "That feels good doesn't it?" I asked her.

She started grinding her pussy against my hand as the juices leaked onto my fingers. My dick got rock hard that instant. So I pulled my hand away from her and started unzipping my pants. "Come suck on this dick." I instructed her.

As she slid to the floor to get on her knees we heard the doorknob on the front door rambling. My heart stopped instantly. Shocked by this, she and I looked at each other. "Oh my God! That's my husband." She panicked and jumped to her feet.

I immediately jumped to my feet as well. But I didn't know where to go. "Where do you want me to go?" I whispered.

She grabbed me by my hand and led me towards a nearby closet. "Stay in here." She told me after she pushed me inside. Three seconds after she closed the closet door the front door opened.

"Hey baby, whatcha' doing back so soon? I thought you weren't coming home until tomorrow." I heard her say. I swear this bitch really knew how to put on an act. Her voice was cheerful as hell. That role she was playing showed me exactly how scandalous she was.

"My company canceled the leadership conference for tomorrow so I just decided to surprise you by coming home early." I heard him say. He sounded like he was a big guy. His voice was strong and it had depth.

"Let me get that for you," she said. I assumed she must've been talking about his coat or his luggage.

"No, I got it honey." He told her and then I heard footsteps as they passed the closet I was hiding in. I saw a shadow walk by but I wasn't able to zoom in on his stature. I wanted to be fully aware of what I was dealing with just in case I had to defend myself. I knew that if a nigga was hiding in my fucking closet I'd put a bullet through his skull. That was blatant disrespect to the max. And I wouldn't be able to come back from that one.

"Have you checked the front desk to see if we had mail?" he asked her.

"No, not yet. And that's because I just got out of the shower."

"Okay, don't worry. I'll run down there and check because I'm looking for this media kit I ordered a few days ago while I was in Chicago."

"Well would you stop by the fitness room to see if any of the treadmills are available?" she said.

"Sure I can." He said.

I heard Brandi and her husband walking around their apartment making small talk until he finally left. I was only in the closet for about five minutes but it felt like I had been in here for hours.

Immediately after the front door closed I heard Brandi lock it and then I heard running in the direction of the closet. She swung it open. "Come on, let's go." She said, panting.

"Aren't you going to make sure he's gone first?" I asked her. I was definitely ready to get out of there. But the last thing I wanted to do was run into that cat while I was leaving his crib. What would I be able to tell him to keep him from swinging on me? See men were entirely different from women. When shit wasn't right we pulled out our pistols first and asked questions last. So you see, it was very important for me to do shit right. I wasn't tolerating it any other way.

"Yes, but stay close behind me so I can tell you when to go."

"A'ight," I said and followed her to the front door.

Once again my fucking heart rate picked up like I was scared or something. And I couldn't figure out why. I was a coldhearted nigga and didn't give a fuck about anyone outside of my family. I killed at will and I left people dead in the streets to leave messages to all parties involved. So I guessed the old me would rear it's ugly head when the time presented itself.

"I don't see him so come on and go now," she instructed me after she peeped her head out the front door.

I didn't wait for her to say another word and raced into the hallway. "Call me when you can," I heard her say as I fled down the hallway. All I thought about was getting back to my apartment to re-group.

There's nothing like coming out on top.

Chapter Twenty-Three
Minus One

I had been in every store on the block and I didn't see Malika in any of them. I thought about calling Reggie and telling him what was going on but I knew he was with that chick Brandi so I decided to wait. Most importantly, I didn't want to cause a scare for anyone, especially my mother. She'd lose her fucking mind if I went back to her apartment and told her that I hadn't found Malika after being gone for a whole damn hour. But then I realized that I couldn't risk being out here longer than I had. I was a wanted woman. That in itself meant I needed to protect my own ass. And that's exactly what I did.

I dreaded going back to my parents' apartment. I dreaded it even more to give my mother the bad news. Unfortunately for me, my mother and Reggie were both sitting in the kitchen talking. She had just microwaved him a plate of leftovers from the previous night. "Did you she where she went?" my mother asked the moment she saw me.

"No," I said. I knew it was barely audible. I didn't even feel my lips moving.

Reggie stopped chewing his food. "You talking about Malika?" he blurted out.

I nodded my head.

"What do you mean no?" my mother became concerned. I heard it in her voice.

"I'm telling you that by the time I got down to the first floor she disappeared when she got outside."

"Whatcha' mean she disappeared? How can a fucking pregnant woman disappear?" Reggie barked. He was definitely getting angrier by the second.

"Look, when I got downstairs I asked the guy at the desk did he see a pregnant woman get off the elevator? And he said no. So, when I went outside the doorman told me that he saw her walk east towards the bus stop. But when I walked that way I didn't see her. And I searched every store and restaurant on the block."

Reggie just sat there with this clueless facial expression. I could tell that his mind was going one hundred miles per minute but I couldn't figure out what he was thinking. My mother on the other hand began to panic. She slung the oven mitten she had on her hand onto the table and stormed out of the kitchen. "We've got to go find her." She said as she rushed down the hallway.

Reggie stood up from the kitchen chair. "No, mom, you stay here. Me and Naomi will handle it."

The shit is about to hit the fan!

Chapter Twenty-Four

Vengeance Is Mine

After I announced that I was going to go and find Malika my mother raced back down the hallway. "Son, please don't do anything to her. Just bring her back here when you find her." She pleaded.

"Yeah, okay." I said, even though I didn't mean it. I didn't have any plans to bring Malika back to my mother's place. And I couldn't tell her that either. My main objective was to get her alone so I could have a few words with her. It had been a little over two weeks since I hit her and it's been the same amount of time since she last stayed at the apartment with me. So, the buck stopped here. I was not accepting anymore of her bullshit. That ship had sailed.

I recruited Naomi to help me look for Malika. On our way out of the apartment we ran into Foxx and Damian. "Where you guys going?" Foxx asked me and Naomi.

"Malika left out of here over an hour ago and we're going to go and look for her." I told him.

"Wait while I put this money away and I'll go with you." Foxx said.

"Yeah, me too." Damian also agreed.

"Was everything straight?" I asked Foxx. I wanted to know was he able to pick up all the money that nigga Keith owed us.

"Oh yeah, we're good."

"Okay, well you and Damian go handle that situation with George and me and Naomi will take care of this."

"Are you sure?" Foxx asked me.

"Yeah, I'm sure. Now go and take care of that thing for us. We can't let one monkey stop this show." I told Foxx and Damian.

"I feel you," Damian said.

"All right, well if something changes, call me." Foxx insisted.

"I will."

I walked out into the hallway while Naomi said a few words to Damian. After I heard them kiss I heard some whispering. I couldn't make out what they were saying but at this point I didn't care. I was more worried about where Malika was. I started thinking all sorts of things while I stood before the elevator. My first thought was that she may be in labor and made her way over to a nearby hospital. Then I thought about the possibility that she could be using someone else's cell phone and calling New York now. I had to admit my blood started boiling at the thought of her calling New York. I swear on my unborn child that if I found out that that bitch was calling New York, I'm gonna fuck her up on sight.

Finally Naomi joined me at the elevator. When the bell rang and the door opened she and I got on it and pressed the button for the first floor. "You don't have your gun with you, right?"

"Nah, I left it at my apartment."

"Good. I would hate for it to fall out while you're arguing with Malika. That wouldn't be a good look at all."

"I thought about it. That's why I didn't go back to my place to get it."

Finally we made it to the first floor and when the door opened my heart crumbled into my stomach when I saw Malika standing before Naomi and I with a white woman and man. I swear I didn't know whether to close the elevator door or make a run pass them. I looked at Naomi to get a queue from her but she had a blank facial expression.

"Are you getting on?" the white man asked Malika.

Malika turned around and looked at the man and said, "Yeah, I'm getting on."

A couple seconds later she walked onto the elevator slowly and when she moved out of the white man and woman's way I saw that they were holding hands. Naomi saw it too. "Are you two getting off?" the white man asked me.

"Nah, we're staying on." I told him.

Malika pressed the button for our floor while the white couple pressed the third floor button. Everyone in the elevator including myself remained quiet. All kinds of thoughts ran through my head. I thought about her calling New York and telling her family all kinds of shit. I pictured her telling her mother where we were. I even pictured her telling her mother that she would get back in contact with her once she had the baby. And boy did those thoughts have my fucking blood boiling. This bitch was more of a headache to me than anything. She was definitely going against the grain and that wasn't my idea of loyalty. I figured either she'd conform or she had to go.

Immediately after the white folks got off the elevator I grabbed Malika by her shirt collar. "Where the fuck you been?" I asked her. Adrenaline rushed through my entire body.

"Get off me!" she yelled.

"No, Reggie. Not here. This is not the place for that." I heard Naomi but her words went through one ear and right out the other.

I totally ignored her. "Answer me right now!" I demanded as I held a tight grip around Malika's shirt collar.

"Reggie this elevator has a camera." Naomi pointed out.

"Yeah, you dumb fuck! Listen to her before your silly ass get locked up." Malika snapped. She was literally talking a lot of shit to me. I didn't know this bitch had balls.

As much as I wanted to punch Malika in her other eye I released the grip from her collar. Naomi was right when she said that this wasn't the place. I knew that if I continued to rough her up in front of this camera I was going to bring some unnecessary heat on myself and possibly my family, so I backed off. Well at least for now.

The elevator doors opened when we reached our floor. When Malika got off I followed her while Naomi followed me. But when Malika tried to make a run for my parents' apartment I threw a monkey wrench in her plans and escorted her to our apartment. She resisted immediately and started screaming to bring attention on herself. "Get off me Reggie! Get off me!" she yelled.

Naomi looked around to see if anyone opened their doors but no one did. "She's gonna have to cut that shit out before someone hears her." Naomi said.

"I ain't cutting shit out! So, mind your business bitch!" She roared.

"Malika, why you making all this noise? Whatcha' trying to get me locked up?" I asked her.

"If I was I would've called the police when you hit me in my fucking eye." She spat. She was still talking loud and resisting me. She tried to pry my hands from her wrist but I wasn't letting go. I needed to get her into our apartment and that's what I intended to do.

Realizing that my approach wasn't working with this dumb ass chick I turned on the charm and persuaded her to come with me. At first she wasn't buying it, but after sixty long seconds of convincing her that I would let her go back to my parents' apartment after she talked to me at our apartment for five minutes, she finally went for it.

I waved Naomi off. "Go ahead and we'll meet back up in about five minutes." I instructed her.

"All right," she said and walked towards my parents' spot.

Malika walked ahead of me and after we got inside of the apartment I closed the door and locked it. She walked straight back to our bedroom. I followed behind her and thought to myself that this was good. Everything was working in my favor. With all the anger and rage I had built up inside of me, I knew at any moment I would be able to release it without anyone hearing it.

She went into our bedroom and started taking clothes from the walk-in closet. Her back was facing me when I walked into the bedroom behind her. "Are you gonna tell me where you been all this time?" I asked her as I approached her.

I took a walk. She said as she continued to take clothes from the closet.

Where did you go? I pressed the issue. I wasn't about to let her off the hook that easy. According to Naomi, she had been gone for over an hour. So, she definitely had some explaining to do.

Before Malika could attempt to explain her whereabouts my cell phone rang. When I looked at the caller ID and noticed that it was Brandi calling me I pressed the END button and put the phone back in my pants pocket.

I'm Forever NEW YORK'S FINEST

Malika finally turned around. Why didn't you answer your phone? She asked me.

Don't worry about who called me. You just tell me where the fuck you been at for over an hour? I roared. She didn't need to be concerned about who called me. She needed to worry about herself right now.

So why is it that I don't need to worry about who called you? It seems strange that you ended the call. You would never end a call if it came from your family or someone you're doing business with.

Look Malika, don't get off the subject. Tell me where the hell you been?

Tell me who just called you and I will tell you where I've been. She said and then she cracked a half smile.

Seeing that she was taking me for a joke I had had it with her and I completely lost my cool. I lunged back and threw the hardest blow/to her face. I aimed for the same eye that I hit the last time. And when my fist connected with her face she fell back into the closet and bumped her head against the wall. She screamed to the top of her voice. Somebody help me! He's trying to kill me! She cried out.

Shut the fuck up bitch! Shut up! I snapped as I gritted my teeth. Her voice was making my skin crawl and I wanted her to close her mouth. But she wouldn't. So, I placed both of my hands around her neck and started squeezing it. At this point I not only wanted her to shut up I wanted her to stop breathing. She was

KIKI SWINSON

a loose cannon and I knew that she was going to be my downfall. She made it very clear that she wanted to create my demise. And I couldn't have that.

I also knew that when I eventually let her up, she was going to leave me. And I couldn't have that either. "Let me go! You fucking psycho!" she managed to utter from her lips as her face turned pink and blue. I couldn't believe it. This bitch was still talking shit to me. It seemed like this nightmare was never going to end. And it became crystal clear that she had to go. So without giving it much thought I applied more pressure around her neck causing her to lose consciousness. I wanted this bitch dead. And to accomplish this mission I had to close off her oxygen supply, which was exactly what I did.

First she started choking uncontrollably as she kicked her legs. And when her eyes rolled into the back of her head her legs stopped kicking and before I knew it the bitch stopped moving altogether.

I didn't release the grip from her neck until I was sure she was dead. "Where ever you were, you won't live to talk about it now." I said to her as I let her go. After I stood to my feet I looked at her lifeless body from head to toe and then I spit on her. Nothing about her made me feel any kind of remorse. She was a fucking demon just like my dead wife Vanessa. So I felt like she got what she deserved.

I was on my way out of the bedroom when I heard a knock on the door. I froze for a second trying to figure out whether to answer it or not. For all I knew, someone could've called the police. But when I heard a woman's voice and realized that it was Naomi, I rushed to the door and opened it. "I thought you were someone else." I said to her.

"Why are you sweating so bad? And where is Malika?" she asked me as she peered over my shoulders.

"She's in the bedroom," I told her.

"What is she doing?" Naomi's questions continued.

"She ain't doing nothing."

"Whatcha' mean she ain't doing nothing?"

"She's dead." I finally told her.

Naomi gave me the look of fear. She looked like she didn't no whether to stay here or run. "Whatcha' mean she's dead Reggie? What did you do to her?" she finally spoke.

"We were arguing and then when she got smart with me I choked her."

Naomi pushed me to the side and sprinted back to the bedroom. I ran behind her. I got there just in time to see her cover her mouth with her hands. "Oh my God! Reggie is she dead for real?" she asked, her voice started cracking.

"Yeah, she's dead." I replied nonchalantly.

Naomi dropped down to her knees to get a closer look at Malika. I watched her grab Malika's wrist and check her pulse. "Reggie, she's not breathing." She said.

"I know." I said as I continued to stand there.

"What are we going to do?" she asked me as tears fell from her eyes.

"I was gonna see if Damian could help me take her body out of here before she starts stinking up the place."

"What about the baby? The baby could still be alive."

"If you ain't gonna cut my baby from her stomach then there's nothing else to dicuss."

"So, you're just gonna leave her like this?" Naomi's cry started getting louder.

"Look, you need to calm the fuck down before somebody hears you." I snapped. I had just murked Malika for getting loud with me and now Naomi was trying to pull the same stunt.

Naomi stood back on her feet. "I can't stand here and watch you disregard my niece or nephew like this."

"So, you think I don't give a fuck about my baby?" I asked sarcastically.

"If you do, you got a fucked up way of showing it."

"Listen Naomi, I wanted my baby just as much as that bitch. But she was starting to bring heat to my family. So, I had to make a crucial decision. And unfortunately my baby got caught up in the crossfire." I tried to explain. I really wanted Naomi to know that I wasn't that fucked up in the head that I didn't consider my baby. I wished my baby was already born before this shit happened. But it didn't work out that way, so we just got to move forward.

"What are you going to tell mom?" Naomi asked while the tears continued to fall from her eyes.

"I haven't figured that out yet. But, I'll think of something." I began to say. "Right now, I'm gonna need you to call Damian over here so he can help me figure out how to get rid of her body."

"You're gonna have to wait until he comes back. Him and Foxx already left to go and see George. And besides, I don't have my phone with me. I left it at mom's place."

"Fuck! I forgot about their meeting." I said as I scrambled to pull my phone from my front pocket. When I finally had it in my hand I turned it around so I could dial Damian's number myself and immediately realized that I hadn't disconnected Brandi's call when she called me over fifteen minutes ago.

I instantly got sick to my stomach because I knew she heard everything that had just went on inside my bedroom. Without saying a word I showed Naomi that the talking time on my phone had been running for fifteen minutes and four seconds. And when Naomi realized that Brandi could have heard me choking the life out of Malika her knees started shaking. I placed my finger over my mouth to let her know that I needed her to be quiet. And after I did that, I placed the phone to my ear in hopes to hear something. For the first several seconds it was completely quiet. But then out of nowhere I heard tiny footsteps. I knew that it couldn't be any one but Brandi so I said, "Hello."

Instead of responding to me, the phone went dead.

"What happened? Did she just hang it up?" Naomi asked.

"Yeah, she did."

"Do you think she heard everything that went on with you and Malika?"

"Yeah, I know she heard it."

"So, what are you going to do? She could be calling the police right now. And if she said she heard someone getting killed, those cops are going to fly over here. And they're gonna come prepared too." Naomi asked frantically.

"Well, that means that she's gotta die too." I told her.

"Oh my God Reggie! How are you going to do that? That girl isn't going to let you in her house." Naomi panicked.

"We'll see about that." I told her. And then I went to the dresser drawer to get my gun.

"So, you're gonna shoot her?"

"Nah, I ain't gonna shoot her. This is gonna help me get through her front door." I told her and then I headed out my apartment.

One down, two to go!

CHAPTER TWENTY-FIVE
Leave No Witnesses

I had one hundred and one million thoughts race through my mind after I left Reggie's apartment. I didn't know whether to help him cover up Malika's murder or run for my own freedom. I knew Reggie had lost his fucking mind but how could I go against him? Reggie had a strong personality and he'd kill at will so he wasn't the type of person anyone would challenge. "What are you going to say when you knock on her door?" I asked him immediately after we entered into the hallway.

"I'm gonna need you to come with me." He said while he locked the door to his apartment.

"What do you want me to do?" I asked him. I wasn't trying to go with him so he could kill this chick Brandi. I wanted no parts of it. But there was no way I could turn my back on him right now. So I went against my better judgment and walked with him to Brandi's apartment.

"I'm gonna need you to knock on her door."

"And say what?"

"Her husband is there with her so he might answer the door. And if he does I want you to act like you're looking for someone else."

"Oh my God! Her husband is there too?" I asked. My heart sunk into the pit of my stomach.

"Yeah, he came home a day earlier than she expected so we're gonna have to deal with him too." He told me as we walked by the elevator.

"Where are we going?"

"We're gonna take the stairs. Don't want the elevator camera to caught us getting off on her floor." he replied.

My hearted continued to race as we entered into stairwell. The air in there was tight and the steps were smaller than usual. It only took two flights of steps to get to Brandi's floor. Reggie opened the door to the hallway and looked in both directions to see if the coast was clear. "Come on, let's go." He said and then we raced into the hallway.

Reggie led the way to Brandi's door. The closer we came to her apartment the more petrified I became. I wasn't built for this type of shit. I organized drug deals and traveled with huge loads of cocaine and heroin. Killing people wasn't what I had signed up for. But once again, how could I walk away knowing these people could help put my brother behind bars? So I was literally forced to stand by my family regardless of how fucked up the situation was.

"Knock on the door and ask for Brandi if the husband answers." He whispered.

"What if she answers the door?" I whispered back to him.

"Ask for her husband."

"What's his name?"

"I don't know. Just ask her is her husband home?"

"Okay," I said.

I tiptoed to the front door and tapped on it very lightly. I did this to prevent anyone other than Brandi and her husband from hearing me. I heard some footsteps as they approached the door on the other side. "Who is it? I heard a man ask me.

I tried to open my mouth and say something but I couldn't. Reggie waved his hand to get my attention while he stood alongside of the door. "Ask him is his wife home? And hurry up before somebody comes." he whispered.

"Is your wife home?" I managed to utter from my lips.

"Who can I say is asking?" he questioned me.

"My name is Christina and I live on the second floor. I got her mail by mistake." I said. I couldn't believe how easily the lie came out of my mouth. For a moment, I almost believed what I said was true.

Two seconds later I heard the guy open the door. He stood in the doorway I assumed to get the mail I told him I had. This guy had to be at least 6'1 and over 400 lbs. I knew Reggie had never laid eyes on this guy because if he had, he would've thought twice before we came here. He smiled at me and said, "I guess someone downstairs isn't doing their job properly."

Before I could respond to the guy Reggie pulled his pistol from his waist and rushed him. After Reggie mushed the man in his face with his gun, he pushed him back into his apartment. "Wait....wait....hold up! What's going on?" the guy said. His voice was pretty loud. So, I closed the door before anyone would get a chance to hear him.

"Nigga, shut the fuck up!" Reggie instructed him as he buried his gun into his head.

I followed them into the living room and watched Reggie as he pushed the man back onto his sofa. "You can have anything you want. My wallet is on the night stand in my bedroom." He told us.

"We don't want your money fat boy. Where is your wife?" Reggie said.

"She just left." He replied.

"Nigga, you better not be lying to me." Reggie warned him.

"I'm not. She just left to go to the gym."

Reggie and I looked at each other. "Go check the bedroom." He instructed me.

I rushed into the bedroom trying to be careful not to touch anything. I used my shirt to open the bedroom door because it was closed. I searched every area of that room. I even looked underneath the bed and the closet and she wasn't there. On my way out of the bedroom I heard a crackling sound. I stopped to see if I'd hear it again, but I didn't. That didn't stop me from going back into the room though. I knew I had searched every crack and crevice. But then it dawned on me that I didn't look in the top part of the closet. So when I went back and took another look I saw Ms.

Brandi hiding in the back of the closet behind a long trench coat. She was hunched over with her face buried in her kneecaps. She looked really pitiful to say the least. "Get up," I said.

She got up slowly from the floor of the closet. "Please don't hurt me." She pleaded softly. Her words were barely audible.

"Did you find her?" Reggie yelled from the living room.

"Yes, I got her." I yelled back to him.

After she came completely out of the closet I sent her into the living room with Reggie. "She's coming your way now." I yelled.

Before I walked away from the closet I noticed something on the floor. I peeped my inside and realized that she left her cell phone on the floor. I reached down and picked it up. I went into her call log and noticed that she had just made two out going calls. The first call was to Reggie and the second call was a 911 call. Once again my heart rate shot up to a high speed. I had to make Reggie aware of this. So, I rushed back into the living room. When I got there Reggie had Brandi sitting on the sofa next to her husband. He was making wise cracks at them. "You are one stupid ass nigga," I heard him say, "while you were trying to save her from me, I had already had her. Did she tell you how long I've been fucking her while you were working out of town? Oh yeah, I was also hiding in your hall closet when you came home early today?"

Brandi's husband looked at her like he wanted to kill her. I quickly intervened. "Look, whatever you're about to do, do it now because while she was hiding in the bedroom closet she called 911."

"How long ago did she make the call?" he asked me.

"It looks like she did it around the time I knocked at the front door."

Reggie looked at Brandi and pointed his gun directly at her. "Oh so now you wanna call the cops on me?"

"Please don't kill me." She begged, holding both hands together.

"Tell me whatcha' said to the police when you called them?" Reggie asked her.

"Don't tell him shit!" the husband barked. He had his chest poked out like he wasn't afraid of Reggie. And why did he do that?

Reggie walked over to the sofa, picked up one of the decorative pillows, placed it against the man's chest and fired his gun twice. I couldn't believe it. The shit happened so quickly.

After Reggie shot the husband, Brandi screamed for dear life. I looked at Reggie to see how he was going to handle her and without saying another word he used the same pillow and mushed her in the face with it. The force behind his hand silenced her immediately and before I knew it, he pulled the trigger once more. Blood and parts of her brain splattered on the back of the sofa and parts of the wall as well. There was no question that she was dead.

"Let's go," he said.

I shoved Brandi's cell phone into my pocket since I had my fingers prints all over it and then I exited the apartment after Reggie.

Were we the next Bonnie and Clyde?

Chapter Twenty-Six
Operation Clean House

I hadn't planned to kill anybody while I was here in Denver but Brandi and her husband didn't leave me any choice. I was taught a long time ago that a nigga would surely sign his death certificate if he left any witnesses alive to talk. It didn't matter how much they'd swear to keep their mouths closed because if the cops put enough pressure on them, they'd sing like a canary.

Naomi and I took the stairs again. "I want you to go to mom's place and tell her to pack her and Foxx's shit because we gotta go." I told her.

"What are you about to do?" she asked me.

"I'm going back to my place and grab my things."

"Where do you want to meet?"

"I'm not sure. So, I'll call you in about fifteen minutes."

"Okay. Well be careful." She said and then she ran in the opposite direction as me.

When I got back inside of my apartment, I ran into the bedroom where my things were. I knew I couldn't leave without my fake ID's and passports. Those things were important documents that I couldn't let the cops get their hands on them.

On my way back out of the bedroom I took one last look at Malika and then I looked at her stomach. I shook my head at the mess I made because I knew I would never have another conversation with her. And I knew that I'd never play with my unborn child. Why couldn't she just be Team Reggie? Why did she go against me for her family? If she hadn't crossed me we'd be together right now. But no, she had to be a dirty bitch like Vanessa. I bet she's wishing she would've had my back now. It's too late though. So, I guess I'll see her on the other side.

When I turned to leave the bedroom I saw Malika's Chanel handbag on the edge of the bed so I snatched it up. I figured I'd have an advantage if the cops didn't have any identification on her when they found her. It would make their job a whole lot harder trying to find out who she was.

Fuck the POLICE!

CHAPTER TWENTY-SEVEN

We Gotta' Go!

"**M**om we gotta go now," I said in a panic.

"Does your father know about this?" my mother asked me. She stood at the entryway of the kitchen with the most puzzled expression she could muster up.

"Yes, he knows about it." I lied. I knew if I told her the truth, she wouldn't budge.

"Where are we going?" she wanted to know.

"Away from here. Dad told me to get you and you guy's things out of here and he'll call us with further instructions." I urged her.

"Well okay," she finally said and raced towards her bedroom.

"While you're getting you and dad's things together, I'm gonna go to my apartment and get me and Damian's things." I said and then I grabbed her cell phone from the coffee table in the living room.

"All right," she replied.

I sprinted out of my parents' apartment and made a run for mine. I raced into the stairwell and when I started going up the first flight I heard a ton of footsteps coming up the stairs below me. "Secure each floor," I heard a militant voice say.

Panic stricken I moved in fast motion as I climbed the stairs to my floor. I looked ahead and noticed that I only had four more steps to climb and when I did I bailed for the door. Panting my poor heart out I peeped into the hallway and noticed that no one was around so I raced to my apartment door and wasted little time unlocking it. After I got inside I hurried up and closed the door and locked it. I took a couple of steps away from my front door and started dialing Foxx's number from my mother's cell phone. Unfortunately the call went straight to voicemail. "No…no…no…this can't be happening." I said quietly.

My heart started beating erratically and my thoughts became cloudy. I didn't know what to do next. "Come on Naomi, calm down …." I said underneath my breath. Then it hit me to try Damian's phone. Thankfully his call went through. "Mrs. Foxx what's going on? Why are all these cops outside the building?" he said in an alarming way.

"It's me Damian. Naomi…." I whispered.

"Hey baby, what's going on?"

I started sobbing quietly. "Reggie killed Malika, that girl named Brandi he was messing around with and her husband. So, the cops are here looking for him."

"What?! Why the fuck he do that crazy ass shit?" Damian yelled through the phone.

"They got into an argument and Reggie just snapped out. Is my father with you?"

"No, he left me sitting in the car while he went into the building to see what was going on?"

"Well, I'm gonna have to grab our stuff and get out of here before one of the cops recognized me."

"Where are you now?"

"I'm inside of our apartment."

"Where is Reggie and your mother?"

"She's at her place packing up her and Foxx's stuff right now. And Reggie went back to his apartment to get his stuff too."

"Where is Malika's body?"

"It's in Reggie's apartment."

"Well, grab everything you can and meet me at the City Cap Tavern on Bannock Street."

"I've got to go back to my parents' place first."

"No, let Foxx handle that."

"Okay."

Once again the cops are closing in on us.

CHAPTER TWENTY-EIGHT
I Fucked Up!

I managed to get out of my apartment and down to the first floor without getting jammed up. My only problem now was trying to get through the lobby and out of the glass doors. I was stuck in this dark ass utility closet not too far from the elevator. I found myself a nice hiding spot behind two huge ass buffer machines. I tried to make a couple of calls to Damian and Foxx's cell phones but the reception in his closet was fucked up. I couldn't even send out a damn text if I wanted to. And what was even more fucked up was that the battery on my phone was about to die any minute now. I wanted to kick myself in the ass for not charging my phone up earlier.

While I continued to send a text and make calls with the bad reception around me my phone finally died. I knew I was in deep shit then. But then it dawned on me that I had Malika's handbag and she always kept her cell phone in it. She and I had the same exact phone. The cell phone she had didn't work, but she still carried it around to get phone numbers from it. Besides that, I knew I could use her battery to re-charge up my phone.

I immediately pulled her handbag from my duffle bag and felt around in it. I bumped into at least a doz-

en other things before I touched the phone. And when I finally got my hands on it, I pressed down on the screen to get some light from it. Before I turned the phone around to retrieve the battery from it I noticed that Malika had written a message to herself like she was keeping a journal. I pressed down on the notebook option and a letter dated May 3rd, started off by saying: *Me and Reggie had the biggest argument ever. And it was all because of his fucking sister. The bitch saw me using this lady's cell phone and told Reggie that I probably used it to call my mother. And when he asked me about it I told him the truth that I called Tiffany but he didn't believe me and gave me a black eye. I couldn't believe it. He never hit me before. I cried for two days looking at myself in the mirror. And now I regret being pregnant by him. He doesn't deserve me. I wouldn't ever do anything to hurt him or his parents. I only called Tiffany so she could pass on the word to my family that I was doing good and that I will call them once I have the baby. But she didn't answer her phone. So, I left her a voice mail message. I swear this whole trip is like a nightmare and I truly wish I could go back to New York and never see him again. I figure if he thinks that I lied to him then why should I be with him? I guess after I have the baby, I'll ask him where we stand.*
Signing out.....Malika.

I was about to throw up in my mouth after I read this journal message Malika wrote to herself. How fucked up in the head could I have been? She hadn't

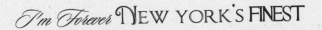

blown the whistle on us. There wasn't any Feds looking for us. She only reached out to a chick from back east so she could get the word out to her family that she was cool. That was it. Wow! I really fucked up my life now. And because of me my baby is dead too. What the fuck was I going to do now?

Can't bring them back now? It's too late.

CHAPTER TWENTY-NINE

No Way Out

"**I**'m gonna need everyone to exit their apartments right now," I heard one of the cops say as he raced down the hallway pass me. "No one is allowed on the elevators. Take the stairs down to the first floor." He continued.

I marched down the flight of stairs with several of my new neighbors. I wore my sunshades and kept my face forward so I wouldn't bring any attention to myself.

"Everyone stay in a single line and exit the stairwell immediately," I heard another cop say as me and the residents made our way into the lobby. I saw Foxx and my mother on the other side of the glass doors so I instantly felt relieved. My heart started beating less and less frequently so I knew I was almost home free.

"Hurry up and get these people out of here right now. We're gonna lock this building down in two minutes." I heard another cop say.

I moved with the crowd heading towards the glass doors when all of a sudden I heard gunshots being fired behind me. BOOM! BOOM! POP! POP! POP! Everyone around me either ran towards the glass doors or fell to the floor. I fell to the floor and when I looked back to see what was going on, I saw

Reggie firing his gun at several of the police officers. My heart immediately went out to me.

While I was on the floor I crawled towards the glass doors. It seemed like I'd never get out of here now. With all the gunshots ringing through-out the lobby everyone went into panic mode.

"Get 'em, he's heading towards the underground garage." I heard someone yell. Sorrow filled my heart that instant. I knew deep down inside that this was the last time I was going to see my brother alive. I knew he made a lot of mistakes and he did a lot of bad things but the thought of losing him weighed heavily on me. What really hurt me was the fact that I couldn't do anything to help him. I knew that if it were me that the cops were gunning behind, he'd risk his life to save mine.

As I watched over a dozen cops race after my brother, a handful of cops started grabbing people and escorting them outside. A female cop grabbed me by the hand. "Come on young lady, we gotta get you out of here so we can apprehend our perp."

I looked up at her. "Do you think they're gonna get 'em?" I asked her.

"Oh yes ma'am. We've got this building surrounded. He's not going anywhere." She replied.

Hearing those words come from her mouth made me sick to my stomach. I didn't want to hear that my brother would be captured or worse, be killed. That didn't sit well with me. And the bad part about it was that I couldn't do anything about it.

KIKI SWINSON

I finally made it outside and was reunited with my mother and Foxx. I told him that I was supposed to meet Damian at the City Cap Tavern. But they were more concerned about Reggie. "Where is your brother?" my mother asked.

I didn't know how to break the news to her so I told her that I thought he was still in the building.

"Your father and I heard gunshots. Do you think those cops were firing at him?"

"I don't know mommy," I said and then I turned my head.

Foxx saw how unsettling I was. He knew I knew more than what I was telling my mother so he pulled me to the side. "Were they shooting at your brother?" he asked me quietly.

I nodded my head.

"Shit!" he said and then he looked at back my mother. Thankfully she didn't hear him. "Do you think they got 'em?" he pressed the issue.

I nodded my head once more.

"Well, come on, we gotta' get out of here." Foxx said.

We walked away from the apartment building we had just moved in a couple of weeks prior. And who would've thought that we'd be leaving so soon. I turned back and looked at the building one last time. It was a sad moment knowing that Malika and my un-born niece or nephew would be coming out of there in a body bag. How was I going to live with myself knowing that I was the one who got her killed?

STAY TUNED
NEW YORK'S FINEST PART 4
COMING SOON

KIKI SWINSON

SNEAK PEEK AT
"SUCKER'S 4-CANDY PART 1"
(E-BOOK SERIES)
AVAILABLE NOW

PROLOGUE

Brooklyn, New York June 2010

"Nigga, you are a broke muthafucka and you ain't got shit to offer nobody!" Celeste Early screamed at the top of her voice. "I'm 'round here struggling to feed my kids and all you wanna do is come up in here and lay up!" She continued as she went toe to toe with her baby daddy.

"Shut the fuck up!" Drake screamed back at her. "Why don't you get your lazy ass up off the system and stop waiting for a man to give you money and get a job, bitch!"

"If you got a fucking job like any responsible man would do and bring some money in this house, instead of hanging out and chasing every piece of ass you see running around town, then I wouldn't have to be on the system!"

This was their normal routine whenever Drake decided to show up at Celeste's house. Ben sat at the edge of his bed listening to yet another argument between his mother and her no good baby father. He rolled his eyes. "Fucking losers, both of them. They

I'm Forever NEW YORK'S FINEST

both need to get a job," Ben said to himself. He often spoke to himself. "Ain't neither one of 'em got no money. That's why my ass hustling now. Fuck 'em. I'ma keep money in my pocket."

Ben pulled out a wad of cash and flipped through the bills. He sniffed the money and then exhaled. He smiled. He was making paper hand over fist now. He had moved up. "Fuck delivering newspapers," Ben said with the smile still on his face.

Just sixteen, Benjamin "Ben" Early had been hustling since he was thirteen. He knew his mother would probably flip if she knew, but in his household it was survival of the fittest. His mother was broke as shit and that was the bottom line. Celeste had him when she was young and she wasn't much for working. Everything Ben got, he got on his own. He realized his mother couldn't possibly miss that he had new clothes, sneakers, fitted hats and always had money in his pocket. Since she didn't say anything, Ben didn't say anything either, primarily because he always bought his baby brother a new pair of kicks when he got himself some. Both Ben and the baby stayed in the latest Jordans and LeBron James sneakers.

Ben was the de facto man of the house. He bought groceries for the house when his mother had prematurely used up all of the food stamp credits on her EBT card. Celeste was horrible about that. She would sell half her food stamps, which meant she only could afford to buy half the amount of food it took to feed a growing boy like Ben and his baby brother.

Ben had found his own way to get food. He learned to make his own paper and buy his own food at an early age.

"Two stacks!" Ben whispered excitedly as he put the rubber band back around the wad of money he had pulled out. Excited about counting his money, he had filtered out the noise coming from his mother's bedroom for a while. "Gotta get this dope bagged up and hit the block," Ben said to himself. He wasn't trying to stay in the house much longer.

"Stupid bitch!" Ben heard Drake yell, once again interrupting his thoughts.

Ben shook his head trying to ignore Celeste and Drake as long as he could. He wondered whatever attracted them to each other. He pulled out a medium sized baggie of dope. Ben had just picked up the bag from Deezo, the dude he sold for and who had told him to go home and bag it up. Deezo had told him to make nicks and dime size bags out of the package.

Ben was excited. He had finally graduated to having his own package and not just doing hand-to-hand for other dudes. He had also moved up from straight cheap ass crack to heroin, which was making a strong comeback in the hood.

"You're a trifling ass bitch anyway Celeste!" Drake screamed.

"Yeah, and you're a broke ass nigga with a little ass dick!" Celeste screamed back.

Ben shook his head. He was getting angrier by the minute with all the commotion. "I gotta get outta this house," he mumbled, getting ready to start bagging his shit so he could bounce. BAM! Ben's concentration on his task at hand was interrupted. He jumped when he heard something slam.

"Ahhh!" his mother screamed. BAM! The sound of thumping and banging came again.

"I know this nigga ain't up in here hitting on my moms," Ben said to himself.

"Bitch!" Drake hollered. WHAP! Ben knew he heard a slap.

"Oh, hell naw!" Ben huffed.

"Get off of me!" Celeste screamed at the top of her lungs.

Ben jumped up. Just then his baby brother, Keon, came waddling into his room. Keon had a look of terror on his face and he threw his arms up for Ben to pick him up.

WHAP! Ben heard another slap. He threw his drugs into an open nightstand drawer and scrambled out of his bedroom, headed for his mother's room. He ran pass his baby brother, leaving the baby standing in his bedroom whining.

"I'm coming right back Keon!" Ben said as he ran to help his mother.

"Get off me! Agghh!" his mother screamed.

Ben kicked Celeste's locked bedroom door, but the door didn't bulge. "Open this door!" Ben screamed from the other side.

"You wanna talk about me bitch!" Drake growled.

Ben could hear his mother gasping for breath. This nigga is choking her! Ben's mind raced. He kicked the door again, this time with all his might. The door flew open with a bang and the doorknob hit the wall.

"Get the fuck off my moms, you punk ass nigga!" Ben screamed, grabbing Drake's shirt. Standing five eleven, Ben was almost as tall as Drake.

"What? Mind your business, this between me and your moms," Drake barked, shaking himself free of Ben's grasp as he finally let Celeste go. She was rolling on the bed holding her neck trying to catch her breath.

"Get the fuck outta my crib!" Ben gritted, stepping close to Drake and getting up in his face. "You don't help out in this place, you ain't shit. Get the fuck out!"

Drake poked his chest out, equaling Ben's status. Celeste finally caught her breath and got up to step between them. She didn't want her son and her baby daddy to fight.

"Wait—" she started to say something, but her words were interrupted. Before she could say another word screams cut through the air. They all froze. Celeste's eyes stretched wide.

"That's Keon!" she screamed. They all whirled around. "Keon?" she called out, kicking off her slippers and running towards her boys' bedroom. Ben was right behind his mother and Drake was on his heels.

"Ahhhhh!" Celeste belted out when she crossed the kids' bedroom door. The baby was flopping on the floor and foaming at the mouth. His eyeballs were completely rolled up into his head and his body jerked horribly.

"Keon! Oh my God!" Celeste let out a bloodcurdling scream.

"What the fuck!" Drake screamed as well, running over to Celeste and Keon on the floor.

With her hands trembling fiercely, Celeste hoisted the baby's limp body off the floor. Baby Keon had stopped moving and his eyes were still rolling. White foam continued dribbling out of his lips.

Celeste rose from the floor and started running with Keon still in her arms. There was no phone in the house. "Somebody call 911!" she hollered as she tried rocking the baby back to consciousness. "Keon, wake up baby!" she repeated as she ran towards the front door. "Help me! Oh God! Keon!".

Drake fumbled with his cell phone, dialing 911 as fast as he could. His car had just got repossessed so they had to wait on 911 to send an ambulance. Celeste was going crazy outside their apartment, with Keon still in her arms.

"Keon!! Wake up baby!" she continued to plead with her baby as she tried shaking him back to life.

Ben was paralyzed with fear.

"What the fuck is goin' on?" Drake huffed, grabbing Ben by the shoulders trying to find out what happened. "What happened to him?" Drake screamed at Ben.

"I . . . I don't know," Ben lied, his eyes opened as wide as they could go.

Drake raced back outside when he heard the ambulance sirens. Ben went back into his bedroom and stood there staring down at the nightstand drawer he had left open. He tightened his fists. Like a robot, Ben reached into the drawer and picked up his baggie of dope. It was more than half empty. In fact, there was just a dusting of the drugs left. It looked as if Baby Keon had spilled the dope, gotten it on his hands and put his hands into his mouth. It was high grade uncut heroin. A small amount of the drug could've put a grown ass man six feet under.

Ben was supposed to get fifteen stacks for the bundle he had once he broke it down, cut it and bagged it into nicks and dimes like Deezo had told him to do. Now he had to get rid of what wasn't spilled out all over the floor. He couldn't let his mother find out that he had dope in the house and left it around for the baby to get. She would break his neck if she ever knew about it. He started wiping up the rest of the powder with his hands. His heart was racing like crazy and he was sweating now.

"What the fuck I'ma tell Deezo," Ben whispered to himself. His stomach cramped up. He was thinking about the consequences that might come from Deezo for this one. But he was also very worried about the condition of his baby brother. Ben could hear his mother outside screaming as the ambulance sirens pierced his ears. Ben continued to frantically clean up the powder. He had to get the drugs out of the house right away.

"Ben! What the fuck you doing? Let's go, the ambulance just left!" Drake boomed from the door-way.

"I'm not going. I . . . I can't see him like that," Ben said nervously.

"Fuck you, lil nigga!" Drake cursed. He didn't have time to even see what Ben was doing. Drake left and Ben felt like somebody had just kicked him in the heart. He was scared and nervous. He didn't believe in God, but he started to pray that Keon didn't die. That occupied one part of his brain. The other part was wor-ried about how he was going to make the money back for the package. Deezo was expecting some loot off the package as well.

When Ben had gotten all of the drugs cleaned up, he left the house. With the money he had counted prior to the incident in his pocket, he hailed a cab and went to the hospital. Ben ran into the emergency room en-trance and looked around for his mother and Drake. He spotted Celeste sitting in a chair rocking back and forth and Drake was standing up with a seriously an-gry look on his face.

"What did they say?" Ben asked his mother nervously. She looked up at him with swollen eyes.

"They are working on him, Ben . . . he can't die Ben. What happened in there?" Celeste cried, looking at her oldest son pitifully.

"I don't know," Ben lied. "I came out there to get this no good nigga off you and I left Keon in the room. I thought he was gonna follow me out the room. I was only gone for a minute, Keon was only in there for a minute." Ben knew the half-truth had to do, he couldn't tell his mother the whole story.

Drake was too distraught to even respond to Ben's smart-ass comment about him being a no good ass nigga. Celeste continued to rock, trying to calm herself down. Then she looked up and saw the doctor walking towards them. She stood up, her knees practically knocking against each other.

"Ms. Early?" the doctor asked.

"Yes," Celeste answered, her voice hoarse from screaming.

"I'm very sorry," the doctor began. "We couldn't save your baby—"

Celeste exploded into ear shattering screams. "Noooo! Please! God! No!" She doubled over like she had been gut punched. She was in great pain. Ben had tears welling up in his eyes too but he tried to play tough. He wanted to be strong for his mother.

Drake punched the wall, and then kicked a waiting room chair. Keon was not Drake's only baby, but it didn't matter. He was still feeling hurt over the death of his son.

"Why?" Celeste screamed.

The doctor held his head down. "Ms. Early, we have to do an autopsy since whatever caused the baby's death happened outside of the hospital. It seemed like the baby's pupils were severely dilated indicating that he may have ingested something into his system," the doctor tried explaining through Celeste's screams.

"Whatcha mean, like he ate some shit that killed him or something?" Drake asked in a gruff tone. That was how he dealt with his grief, he got angry and violent.

"Yes. Like he took in something that poisoned his system or caused him some kind of toxicological shock," the doctor continued using big words none of them could understand.

Ben was silent. His heart was beating out of control.

"You can see him before we take him down," the doctor said.

Celeste was so weak she could hardly walk as they all followed the doctor to the room where Keon lay on a small bed. When they walked into the room there were nurses cleaning up all the papers and tubes and mess from where they had tried to work on the baby to save him.

Celeste opened her swollen eyes. "Agghh!" she hollered when she saw her baby lying there. His little eyes were closed and his cherubic face looked like he was just sleeping. Drake and Ben helped Celeste over to the bed. Her knees buckled. "God! Why! Why my baby?" she continued to cry. She reached out and touched him. His skin was still a little warm.

"You can hold him," one of the nurses said softly.

She picked up Keon's limp body and handed him to Celeste. Celeste cradled the chubby, lifeless toddler against her chest. "Mmmmm," she moaned as she rocked her baby back and forth.

Ben stood close, watching, his mind racing with thoughts. It was his fault. If I had just put the drugs away before I left the room, none of this would've happened, he thought to himself. Now his brother was dead.

Celeste had to almost be peeled away from her baby. Drake had forgotten all about their fight and Ben just stayed quiet. In his head, he kept blaming himself repeatedly. There was no way he could tell his mother what happened. He knew he had to keep his secret to himself—hopefully forever.

The next day, Celeste was asleep. The doctor had prescribed her a sedative so she could sleep without the memories of Keon keeping her up. The loud knocks on the apartment door stirred Ben from his sleep. Drake had left. He was in and out. He didn't really live with Celeste and the kids.

Ben jumped up and looked around as the knocking continued. His heart started racing, thinking it might be Deezo looking for him. Ben listened and heard the knocks again. He got completely up and pulled on a pair of basketball shorts. He rubbed sleep from his eyes and made his way to the door. He looked through the peep hole, and felt a sigh of relief when it wasn't Deezeo.

"Who is it?" he screamed.

"It's the police! We're looking for Celeste Early," a voice filtered through the door.

Ben's heart started hammering in his chest. "She sleep!" he yelled back.

"Wake her up. This is about her baby, Keon. We need to speak to her immediately."

"Shit," Ben said under his breath. He walked to his mother's bedroom, wishing he could undue all of this. Maybe they want to tell her something else, Ben rationalized in his mind. He shook Celeste's shoulder, but she didn't budge.

"Ma!" Ben called her and shook her some more.

"Mmm," Celeste moaned. The sedatives had her in a deep sleep. There was no way with her baby being dead that she would've been able to fall asleep.

"Ma, the cops are at the door. They wanna speak to you," Ben told her.

Celeste fought against how drowsy the sedatives made her feel and opened her eyes. "What?" she asked, still dazed.

"There are cops at the door," Ben repeated himself. "They said they need to talk to you about Keon."

Celeste sat up. "Open the door," she grumbled.

Celeste forced herself to get out of bed. Feeling tired and depressed, she put on her bathrobe and went into the bathroom. She splashed water on her face and looked at herself in the mirror. Her eyes were puffy and looked as if somebody had used her as a punching bag. Celeste didn't care. She could hear the police talking in her tiny living room. She dragged her feet out of the bathroom and went into the living room. Her hair was wild and unkempt on top of her head, and she still looked a little drowsy from the sedatives. "Can I help y'all," Celeste said in a raspy, hoarse voice.

"Ma'am, we need to talk to you about your baby son, Keon Early," the plain clothed cop stated. "The hospital social worker contacted us today."

Celeste looked the cop up and down. Since he wasn't in uniform, she knew he was a detective. That was common knowledge in the 'hood.

"And," Celeste said, moving closer to them.

"Ms. Early, you're gonna have to get dressed and come with us," the detective retorted. "We need to ask you some questions down at the station."

"Questions . . . about what? My son is dead, that's all the answers you need," Celeste snapped, hugging herself tightly.

"Ms. Early, it's important that you cooperate. Your baby's autopsy and toxicology report show that he died of an overdose of heroin," the detective said flatly, showing no emotion or respect for a grieving mother.

Celeste couldn't react. The sedatives had her brain on slow motion. "What? No you making a mistake here officer . . . don't nobody in here take no heroin," Celeste said, her voice firm, yet slurred, with denial.

The other detective walked closer to her. "Well, you look pretty high right now," he said snidely.

"I don't get high!" Celeste growled at him.

"From the looks of things around here, it seems like you might be lying to us," detective number one interjected. They were looking around at the cramped and junky apartment. There were clothes piled up on the couch, dishes spilling out of the sink and the furniture was old, some of it broken down. Celeste wasn't the best at keeping a clean house, but she wasn't on drugs.

"Oh, now being poor means I'm on heroin! I may not have much but I ain't no dope fiend. I know y'all think all us mothers in the 'hood get high, but I got news for you . . . this one don't. Ain't no way my baby got no heroin in his system . . . I don't even allow drugs in my damn house!" Celeste spat.

Ben felt like he was going to faint. Shit! Now they know Keon got to the drugs! Ben screamed in his mind. Now he not only had to worry about what he was going to tell Deezo about the missing package, but the cops were investigating. He felt as if he would throw up.

"Miss, you can get dressed or we can take you down like this," the detective said, his tone nasty and demanding.

Celeste began to cry. "What about my baby? He gotta have a funeral! Y'all arresting me? I can't believe this shit! I can't even grieve for my dead child!" she screamed, shaking her head left to right.

"We want to take you down for questioning. You may also have to submit to a drug test and we'll be back with a search warrant for the house," the detective explained. It was as if they didn't even care about her feelings. Celeste knew that shit meant she was not coming back home. Shaking all over, she dragged her feet towards her bedroom. One of the detectives followed her.

"Can I get dressed in peace?" she growled. He stepped back and stood outside her bedroom door while she pulled on some clothes. Celeste stepped back into the hallway with tears in her eyes. This was like her worst nightmare coming to life.

She looked at Ben with sadness and tears in her eyes. "Ben, how did this all happen?" Celeste asked.

The detectives started escorting her out of the apartment. "You got somebody to take care of him?" the detective asked Celeste, nodding at Ben.

"No, it's just me," she said sadly.

"C'mon boy, you gon' have to come with us too, until we figure out whether or not your mother is coming home," one of the detectives told Ben. Ben just stood there dumbfounded. He knew leaving his apartment with the cops wasn't a good look. Deezo always had people watching.

"Ben, how did all of this happen?" Celeste asked again, looking at him desperate for an answer or any words that could help her figure it all out.

Ben had a simple look on his face. His mind was going a mile a minute. He was thinking about how this all happened—how it all got started.

CHAPTER 1

Three years earlier.

"Oh daddy, yeah, you fuck me so good! Yeah, beat this pussy up! Ohhh, I'm cumming, daddy!" Celeste screamed in ecstasy as yet another one of her boyfriends laid the pipe.

Ben lay in his bed with his arm over his eyes listening to his mother fuck once again. This was nothing new to him. His mother's door had been like a revolving door since he was very young and she was still broke as hell. Ben pulled his knees up to his chest when he felt the hunger pains ripping through his belly again. That made him angry. His mother had all of these dudes in and out, but there was never anything to eat in the house. He turned over onto his stomach thinking that maybe laying on it would help the hunger pains subside. It didn't help one bit. He put his pillow over his head to drown out more sounds of his mother getting her back blown out. "Fucking ho!" Ben cursed, jumping up out of the bed. He could see the sun rising out of his window. It was almost time for him to run his paper route and make some money. That was the only way he would eat. It was far from the first or the fifteenth of the month, which meant Celeste couldn't afford any food.

Ben walked into the small kitchen in the project apartment he shared with his mother. He opened the refrigerator, there was nothing inside but an open can of Budweiser beer. It was the same story in the cabinets, minus the beer. When Ben opened the shabby cabinet doors, inside was bare except for the one or two hungry roaches that ran. He knew this beforehand but it was force of habit to open the refrigerator and cabinet doors with the hope food suddenly appeared.

"Shit, y'all niggas at the wrong house looking for crumbs," Ben said to the roaches. He slammed the cabinets hoping the noise would disturb his mother's groove. It didn't work. She just kept right on doing her thing.

Ben went back in his room and slid on the one pair of sneakers he owned—a beat down pair of Nike Uptowns that used to be white but now looked more like dark brown. Celeste had finally broke down and bought Ben a pair of sneakers about eight months prior. The shits were run down in the back, dirty and starting to rip on top. Ben was embarrassed to wear them to school. At thirteen, while other kids were rocking fly gear, Ben had two pairs of jeans that he played switch-a-round with, two hoodies and a few dingy white t-shirts. That was all his wardrobe consisted of. He had stopped going to school because of the way the kids teased him about his clothes.

As soon as he had turned thirteen, fed up with being hungry, Ben had walked his Brownsville neighborhood trying to find a job. Then he happened upon a new store that had just opened up near Pitkin Avenue. The owner told Ben if he delivered fliers to houses and other stores he would get paid for each one that he got rid of. That worked for a while, but the owner caught on that Ben was just dumping the fliers and coming back to get paid. Finally, Ben graduated to a full-time paperboy route. He would ride his pieced together bike to the Daily News newspaper depot, pick up his papers for the day and make deliveries in nice neighborhoods. Ben was making $100 a week and he thought it was so much money. It was to him. At least he could buy some food. Celeste always had her hands out for a little bit of the money too.

Ben hurried up and got dressed. He was too damn hungry to play around. He needed to do his paper route, get his chips up and get something to eat quickly. He walked to his mother's bedroom door and kicked the bottom of it. "I'm going to work!" Ben yelled to his mother. "Shouldn't tell your ass shit," he said softly to himself.

"A'ight, go make that paper, boy," Celeste replied, giggling at the man she was locked up in the room with.

Ben shook his head in disgust and prepared to leave the house. He picked up his raggedy bike and wheeled it out of his small apartment. Outside, he climbed onto the bike and rode down his block. He passed the usual neighborhood corner boys with their flashy chains and fresh gear. They were out there playing Cee-lo and talking shit, their usual daily routine.

Ben knew they were doing their thing and making money. He slowed his pace when he noticed a candy apple red Cadillac Escalade pulling up to the

group of boys. Ben's heartbeat quickened. He felt a pang of excitement come over him. Everybody knew who drove that boss ass Escalade.

It was Deezo, a big time hustler whose reputation preceded him. Deezo was known to be notorious and he didn't play with his workers or his paper. He was also like the hood's Robin Hood. He would hand out turkeys at Thanksgiving and give kids sneakers and toys at Christmas. Ben had been the recipient of a few of Deezo's generous gifts. Deezo was both feared and revered in Brooklyn. In Ben's assessment, Deezo was the man.

Ben stopped for a minute when he noticed Deezo's ride. He wanted to catch a glimpse of the man he admired so much. He had been looking up to Deezo since he was a little boy. In Ben's eyes, Deezo was more than the man around his way. Deezo had everything, a bunch of fly ass cars, more than one diamond encrusted chain with chunky platinum pieces hanging from them, huge diamond earrings in each ear and every type of designer clothes you could think of. Ben had made a mental note to check out Deezo for a month. Every time he turned around, Deezo had on a different color pair of Prada sneakers to match all of his Yankee fitted caps. Ben used to daydream about being just like Deezo when he got older. The hood's Robin Hood was Ben's role model.

Deezo pulled the Escalade up to the corner and all of the boys stopped what they were doing. Dice stopped flying, the talking stopped and so did the drug sales. It was like the corner boys were in the army when Deezo came through. They all stood up straight and at attention, looking at the Escalade.

"Ayo' Quan, wassup?" Deezo called out from the window of his ride.

Ben had also noted that Quan was the dude in charge of that corner. He was the one who collected on Deezo's loot from the corner boys that Deezo allowed to slang there. Quan walked over to the Escalade and gave Deezo a pound. With the slap of the hands, Ben saw them pass the money.

Smart, Ben thought to himself. He was making notes. Ben wanted to be just like them. Getting mad paper and fly as hell.

"Yo, lil nigga, whatcha' looking at?" one of the corner boys said to Ben after noticing him watching Deezo so closely. Ben stretched his eyes and rode off to do his paper route. Ben turned back one more time before he left the block and he noticed Deezo looking at him. Ben almost crashed his bike when he saw Deezo's eyes on him.

That evening after Ben had finished his paper route, he slung the empty cloth newspaper bag on his bike handlebars and headed home. He was tired and hungry but he was happy to have gotten paid, which meant he had money for food. Ben got to his block and as usual the same corner boys were still out there doing the same thing—slanging them thangs. He pulled his rickety bike up to the side of the store, leaned it against the wall and passed the boys to get into the store. Ben unfolded the five crumpled twenty-dollar bills he had just earned. He was proud of his payday. He went around the store picking up stuff he wanted to eat—a box of Apple Jacks, half a gallon of milk, a pack of Lorna Doone cookies and three bags of barbeque potato chips.

"She better not ask for none of my stuff either," Ben mumbled about his mother. He went to the counter and put his stuff down. "Yo A-rab . . . let me get a hero," Ben called out to the man behind the counter. "I want ham and American cheese, lettuce, tomatoes, mayonnaise, mustard and oil and vinegar." His mouth watered as the man set about making his hero, which would be his dinner. He was sure his mother probably hadn't cooked shit.

As Ben waited for his sandwich to be ready, he glanced out of the store window at the corner boys. He daydreamed for a minute thinking about all the things he would buy if he were in their positions. The first thing Ben thought of was new clothes. Clothes were a big status statement in Brooklyn. Most people in his neighborhood judged you on what you wore and how often you changed to something new.

The storeowner startled Ben when he told him his stuff was ready. He pulled out his bills and paid for his meager groceries. Ben stepped out of the door of the store and just as he did he noticed all of the corner boys starting to scatter.

"Five-O niggas, five -o en route!" one of the boys called out with his hands cupped around his mouth.

Ben looked around in confusion. Then he noticed the cop cars speeding down the streets, flashing lights but without any sirens blaring. The cops were trying to sneak up on the boys, but all corner boys had lookouts. The word had already gotten out and the scrambling had begun. Ben grabbed up his bike and threw his grocery bag into the newspaper delivery bag that hung from his handlebars.

"Yo Shorty, take this and put it in your bag," Quan, the lead corner boy who Ben had seen talking to Deezo, shouted at Ben. Ben's eyes widened as Quan stuffed something into Ben's newspaper bag. "Get the fuck outta here now, Shorty! I'll see you later on about that! I know where you live at!" Quan barked frantically.

Ben nodded at Quan and did as he was told. With his heart hammering wildly in his chest, Ben climbed onto his bike and rode off doing top speed. He turned to look back once and noticed that the jump out boys had all of the corner boys lined up against the wall near the store, including Quan. Ben inhaled deeply and peddled his bike even faster. When he got to his building, he snatched the cloth newspaper bag off his bike and raced into his apartment. He was so nervous his hands shook. He raced pass his mother, who was in the living room with a new boyfriend that Ben was seeing more often now.

"Damn, you don't say wassup?" Celeste called after him.

Ben ignored her. He went into his room and closed the door. He set the newspaper bag down on the floor and flopped on his bed. He was scared to look inside the bag at first but curiosity was killing him. He took out his grocery bag first, and then slowly he peered down into the cloth bag. His eyes lit up and he swore he could feel his blood pressure rising. Ben swallowed hard as he stared at the content of the bag. In the bottom of the bag lay three bundles tightly wrapped in plastic. Ben slowly and reluctantly picked each of the bundles up. One bundle was a bunch of red-capped containers with white rocks in them. The second bundle was a bunch of brown and green grass looking stuff in small baggies and the third bundle was a bunch of tiny baggies with white powder in them. Ben knew all three bundles were drugs—crack, weed and either powdered cocaine or heroin. Although he was thirteen, growing up in the hood afforded Ben a vast street knowledge about drugs.

"Ben! Open this door!" Celeste hollered from the other side.

Ben jumped. He snatched the bundles of drugs and lifted his thin mattress and slid all three bundles under it. Inhaling and exhaling to get his nerves together, he walked over and opened his door. His mother eyed him up and down suspiciously.

"Did you get paid today?" Celeste said, letting her eyes scan his room. Ben sucked his teeth and rolled his eyes. He could not stand his pain in the ass mother when she acted so money hungry.

"Whatcha' was doing up in here with the door locked? Trying to hide ya little bit a money?" Celeste snapped as Ben pushed pass her to go into the kitchen.

"Nah, I ain't hiding nothing from you!" Ben snapped back. He started unloading his little bit of groceries.

"Well, give me what's mine nigga. Ain't no free stays up in here . . . shit your ass getting grown," Celeste told him, sticking her hand out.

Ben did as he was told. He handed Celeste $40 out of the money he had left. That left him with about $30 after he had already spent about $30 on groceries. He acted angry but he wasn't really mad. He didn't mind helping his mother out, she was a single mother with no help from whoever his no good ass father was. However, Ben didn't appreciate it when men came over and he and his mother were hungry and those niggas didn't even help out by buying as much as a loaf of bread. Ben thought his mother was real stupid for giving up her ass to no good niggas for free.

Ben sat down to eat his hero, but when he lifted the greasy sandwich to his mouth he found that he didn't have an appetite. He was thinking hard about the packages under his mattress. He thought he could go out there and sell every bit of those drugs and make good money. He also knew if he did that, Quan and Deezo would surely be looking for him. Ben decided to just wait and see if they ever came to claim what was theirs. After thinking about the drugs, the money and Quan and Deezo repeatedly, Ben finally forced himself to eat his sandwich. He went to bed full and worried. All he could do was hope that things were going to start looking up.

Ben didn't hear from Quan for the entire night. He tossed and turned all night knowing that the package was under his mattress. The next day, he woke up to knocks on his door. Ben scrambled out of his bed and raced to the door before his mother could answer it. When Ben pulled back the door, Quan and Deezo were standing there. Ben almost shit his pants.

"Whaddup Shorty? I came to pick up my shit," Quan said. Deezo stood silently with a serious glare on his face. He didn't look happy.

Ben shook his head up and down absentmindedly, too star struck to even speak. Quan and Deezo stepped inside of the apartment without Ben inviting them in. Ben knew Celeste slept late so he wanted to hurry up and get what they came for before she got up and saw the two biggest neighborhood hustlers in her living room. He rushed to his room, retrieved the three bundles and proudly handed them over to Quan. Deezo kept his eyes on Ben while Quan surveyed the bundles. Ben could feel sweat dripping down his back.

"It's all here Shorty. Good looking out. You did a'ight," Quan said, smiling at Ben.

Ben's shoulders slumped in relief. Although he knew he hadn't taken anything out of the bundles, he was still scared as hell.

"That's wassup Shorty. Here, this is for ya troubles. Look like a nigga could use the help and shit," Deezo said, handing Ben two crisp one hundred dollar bills.

Ben's eyes lit up. "Thank you," he smiled up at Deezo.

"Buy ya self something Shorty. Ya moms be trippin' the way she got this crib looking. This ain't no way for a lil' nigga to live," Deezo commented, turning around to head for the door. Been shook his head agreeing with anything Deezo had to say. "And Shorty, since you did so good with this little job, I got something you can do to make some money if you want to. I'ma see you out there. I might can help you get ya chips up, feel me?" Deezo stopped walking and told Ben.

Ben couldn't stop smiling. He couldn't believe Deezo was offering him a job. He had dreamed about being down with Deezo. When Deezo and Quan left, Ben raced over to the window and watched them get into Deezo's Escalade. He could see all of their bling sparkling against the sun. The whole scene excited Ben. "I'ma have that car when I get older," he said to himself, gripping the money Deezo gave him.

Ben was too excited to eat his Apple Jacks that morning. He rushed and got dressed. He didn't take his newspaper bag or anything else. He left the house, grabbed his bike and headed for downtown Brooklyn. Ben went straight to Footlocker first. He copped a fresh, crisp new pair of white Nike Uptowns. Then he went to several other stores and copped a traditional navy blue Yankees fitted cap, a brand new pair of Sean Jean jeans and a five pack of crisp white tees. He felt good about himself now. He wore his new sneakers right out the store, the same for his jeans and one of the t-shirts. Ben even had enough money to eat a super-sized meal from McDonalds. He felt like a man. No, he felt like the man. He felt independent. It was a feeling Ben wanted to have all the time. He was definitely going to take Deezo up on his offer.

When Ben returned to his hood that evening he rode his bike past the corner store. He was secretly hoping he would run into Deezo or Quan.

"Shorty!" Quan called after Ben. Ben smiled to himself and stopped his bike.

"Yeah," he answered. His prayers had been answered.

"Deezo told me to hook you up son. All you gotta do is go getcha newspaper bag, come get a package and deliver it to a address across the way . . . two stacks is what Deezo paying for the one trip," Quan told Ben.

Ben felt like he would piss his pants. Two hundred more dollars just like that! Ben thought excitedly. "A'ight. I'll be right back," Ben said, excitement lacing his words. He took flight on his bike, and ran into the house in a huff. He scrambled to his room to get his bag. But his activity was interrupted.

"Where you been at?" Celeste said dryly, stepping into Ben's bedroom with her arms folded. Ben stopped like a deer caught in headlights.

"I went to work and then shopping," Ben lied.

"Where you get money to shop?" Celeste asked suspiciously. She always wanted to know every dollar he had.

"I saved it up from the newspaper route," Ben told her impatiently. He didn't know why his mother was sweating him. It was annoying. Ben screwed up his face at Celeste.

She looked at him up and down. "I got something to tell you," she said. Ben gave her a blank stare. He wanted to tell her to get the hell out of his room so he could get his bag and be out. He was preoccupied and full of anticipation for the job he had coming up.

"I'm pregnant. You gon' have a brother or sister," Celeste said dryly.

"And," Ben answered, being a smart ass.

"You too grown for your own good Ben. I'm just telling you. I ain't have to tell you shit," Celeste snapped.

"So you shouldn'ta told me then," Ben said with an attitude. He grabbed his bag and brushed pass his mother bumping her slightly. "Another mouth to feed and she don't even feed me," he mumbled on his way out. He knew whoever his mother was pregnant by was probably not going to be around or help out in the house. This annoyed him even more. Ben snatched his bike and started out the apartment door. He didn't have time for his mother and her bullshit right now.

"Where the hell you goin' at this time with that bag?" Celeste asked.

Ben didn't answer his mother. He felt like she wasn't in any position to question him. Thirteen or not, Ben was the breadwinner in their household.

"Benjamin Early!" Celeste called after him.

Ben let the door slam behind him. He had to get back outside. Quan was waiting on him. "A'ight, I'm back," Ben huffed putting his feet on the ground to stop his bike.

Quan dropped a package into Ben's newspaper bag. "Take this across the way to Howard Houses, there's a kid named Spider waiting on you. Don't fuck this up lil' nigga," Quan warned.

Ben pulled himself up on his bike and was out. He had a new job and it paid more than he could ever dream of making as a newspaper delivery boy.

Two weeks had passed and Ben had made eight deliveries for Deezo. He had more money than he could have ever dreamed of. Each time he earned another two hundred dollars, he would buy another full outfit, complete with fitted cap. Ben started giving Celeste $100 instead of the $40 she was accustomed to getting from his paper route. Celeste was happy as hell. She had only questioned Ben once about where he got the extra money. He told her he had picked up a new route that paid more money, which was not a complete lie. Celeste was satisfied with the answer . . . at least, that is what she told herself.

SNEAK PEEK INTO
"MAD SHAMBLES"
UNEDITED VERSION

CHAPTER ONE
The First Mistake

On this particular school morning Lisa Cooks was sound asleep in her bed. She had engaged in a late nightcap with her new boy Kenny Wells. They were the perfect couple in the sight of a blind man. Lisa was a mother of four children all by different men. Not one of the children's fathers were in her children's lives financially or otherwise, so Lisa had no choice but to depend of the state for everything from food stamps, Medicaid and section eight vouchers. Working a three to eleven shift cleaning bathrooms and vacuuming floors wasn't her cup of tea. She wanted money to come to her easy. So, it didn't take her long before she found a way to beat the system. When she made money on the under the table from doing odd jobs, she neglected to report it to her social worker because if she did, it would jeopardize her getting her food stamps and it would cause concern for her social worker to review her case. And she couldn't afford to have that happen. Not right now in these critical times.

Her second child, Jeffrey had awakened her from her sleep. "Ma," He shouted irritably as he burst into

KIKI SWINSON

her bedroom, which was the master bedroom of their low- income-housing apartment in the rough neighborhood of the Huntersville of Norfolk.

Startled, Lisa awoke noticing who called her name. "What the hell you want Jeffrey? And why the hell did you know before you came busting in my damn room?" She snapped.

"But Ma, I don't have anything clean to wear to school this morning. All my stuff is in the laundry room dirty."

"Whose fault is that?" Lisa yelled back.

"You're my mama right?" Jeffrey asked with a bit of hesitation. "I mean, you would be the one who's suppose to wash everybody's clothes." He continued and waited for Lisa to come back with a rebuttal. Jeffrey may have been ten years of age, but he was a bright young kid and he knew more than what Lisa gave him credit for. Living in the rough neighborhood, Jeffrey has seen everything from prostitution, to old ladies getting robbed at gunpoint. So, to figure out that his mother would be responsible for making sure he had clean clothes to wear to school was easy math.

"Don't be a smart ass! None since you think you got all of the damn answers, take your ass back in the laundry room and think about which one of those dirty ass shirts and pants you gon' wear to school this morning."

"You're gonna make me wear dirty clothes to school?" He pressed the issue. He made it known that he was happy at all.

"Look, I don't care what you wear. I know you better get outta my damn room before you wake up Bernard."

"Wasn't he supposed to be up a long time ago? I remember you fussing at him last night telling him that he had to get up early this morning to go and look for a job. And then you said that a man, who doesn't work, doesn't eat. But, I'll bet that he's going to be the first person at the table eating a big bowl of cereal."

Lisa's face turned bloodshot red. She knew her son was telling the God's honest truth. But the fact that it was coming from a ten year old didn't sit well with her. "Boy, if you don't mind our damn business and get out of my room, I swear I am going to get out of this bed and tear your ass up!" She roared.

"Why you mad at me? You should be mad at him."

Lisa moved to the edge of the bed. "Jeffrey you better get out of my room right now. And I'm not gonna say it again."

"What about my clothes?"

Lisa didn't say another word as she began to get out of her bed. Jeffrey knew that if he gave her a chance to get close to him, that he'd be in big trouble. So, he sucked his teeth and said, "Well, I'm not going to school today."

Steaming from her son's remarks, Lisa watched at he stormed out of her bedroom. She didn't let him get very far because seconds later she followed him into his bedroom. He turned his attention towards her, giving her the most disappointed expression he could muster up. Lisa, who was a fairly attractive, brown-skinned woman who had problems with self-esteem issues because she couldn't keep a man and she was the largest of her other two best friends. In addition to that, she was a high school dropout that was frowned upon by every employer she was interviewed by. The only thing she had going for her was that she knew how to survive on three hundred dollars worth of food stamps a month. And knew how to stretch a dollar. Other than that, her skills set was on zero.

"Why are you just standing there looking stupid? Because your knuckle-head ass is getting out of my house this morning. Clean clothes or not."

"So, you gon' make me wear dirty clothes to school?" He questioned her.

But she ignored him and walked over to his bedroom closet and then she bent down and started rambling through a few clothing items she saw on the floor. "Here is something you can wear." She said and held up a pair of blue denim Levi's."

"But I just wore those the day before yesterday. And anyway, they gotta' mustard stain on one of the pants legs." Jeffrey explained.

"Boy shut up! All you have to do is take a damp washcloth and wipe that stain out. Trust me, it's gonna look good as new."

"But, I just told you that I wore them day before yesterday. Everybody in my class is gonna notice. And then I'm gonna be joked on the entire day."

"Stop acting like a little girl and man up! No one's gonna joke on you. Now take these damn jeans and do like I said. Your bus will be here any minute now."

Instead of Jeffrey taking the pairs of jeans from his mother, he stood there. So she threw them into his face and walked back out of his bedroom. "You think I'm playing with you. But miss that bus and see if I don't go upside your damn head."

"You need to go upside Bernard's head." Jeffrey mumbled underneath his breath as he watched his mother go to the next bedroom.

She knocked on door. "Who is it?" Lisa heard her oldest child Keisha ask.

"It's your mama." Lisa replied. "Are you up and dressed for school?" She continued.

"Yeah, I'm up."

To confirm what Keisha had just said, Lisa opened her bedroom door. It didn't surprise her to still see Keisha still lying in the bed. "What is wrong with you? The truth ain't in your body nowhere is it?" Lisa snapped after she stormed into Keisha's bedroom and ripped the blanket from her body. The sunlight beaming in from the window blinded Keisha's eyes. "Mom, why you do that?" She protested as she placed her pillow over her face.

"Keisha stop acting like a damn drama queen and get your ass up so you can get ready for school."

"But I am up."

"Stop playing with me and get out of this bed." Lisa warned her as she stood over top of her.

Doing just as Lisa demanded, Keisha turned over and got out of the bed. "Now, get it together."

Keisha sucked her teeth. "I am." She whined.

"Well, hurry up because you only have twenty minutes."

"Okay, but can I iron my shirt first?"

"Keisha, you mean to tell me you didn't iron your clothes last night before you went to bed?"

"No."

"And why not? You know the rules of the house." Lisa scolded her.

Keisha sucked her teeth. "I was tired. And besides, I had to finish my homework."

"Your homework. You were tired? Tired of what? You don't do shit but stay on the damn phone all night long talking to those thug ass niggas and those fast ass girls. But, I'll tell you what, keep fucking with them and see how your life turns out. You gon' end up like me living in Huntersville in a fucking section eight apartment messing with niggas who can't rub two damn nickels together to help you pay a light bill."

"No I ain't. I ain't gon' ever mess with the type of guys you be bringing in here."

"I beg your fucking pardon! " Lisa retorted. Lisa was taken aback by Keisha's comment. So, she stood there and waited for Keisha to clean up the mess she just made.

Instead of apologizing to her mother, Keisha sucked her teeth and said, "I ain't got time for his." Less than two seconds later, she stormed out of her bedroom and headed towards the bathroom in the hallway.

Lisa became livid and cursed aloud as Keisha walked away. "You grown ass hussy!"

Keisha mumbled a few words underneath her breathe and though it was barely audible, Lisa heard her. In rage, Lisa stormed out of the bedroom behind her. "I hear you cussing underneath your breath." Lisa yelled. But by the time Lisa made it into the hallway, Keisha had made her way into the bathroom and locked the door. "Open up this damn door now!" Lisa demanded as she banged on the bathroom door with her right fist.

"For what Ma? I didn't do anything wrong." Keisha calmly replied.

"Girl, you better open up this mutha fucking door before I knock it down." Lisa spat back.

Meanwhile Keisha tried to reason with Lisa, Lisa's son Lil' Tony walked up to her and tug on her housecoat to get her attention. "Ma, can I stay at home with you today?"

"No sir! You are getting your ass out of here. I'm gonna help myself to some quiet time today."

"Does that mean Kenny is gonna go look for a job today?" Lil Tony asked his mother. And before Lisa could react to it, Keisha burst into laughter on the other side of the bathroom door.

"Ha…..ha….ha…." Kesha bellowed. "Lil Tony you are crazy." she commented as she continued to laugh.

Furious at Lil Tony, Lisa slapped him across the head and then she screamed to the top of her voice. "Y'all think I'm a damn joke. And why is everybody worried about Kenny getting a fucking job? I know one thing, y'all better stay out of my business before I make y'all regret the day you were born."

Lil Tony stood there in front of Lisa with a non-chalant facial expression. He didn't look fazed one bit. Lisa witnessed it and became irritated with his presence and stormed off. "Y'all better stay away from me this morning before I go off." she yelled.

After Lisa disappeared into another part of the apartment, Keisha cracked opened the bathroom door just enough to see peep her head out. "You sure told mama off," she said and then she chuckled.

"Yeah, and I got smacked upside my head for it too." Lil Tony admitted.

Keisha sucked her teeth. "Oh boy…..man up! She didn't kill you." she continued and then she closed the bathroom door.

"Easy for you to say when you weren't the one getting hit." Lil Tony commented and then he walked off.

Stay Tuned!

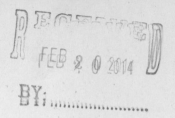
DATE DUE

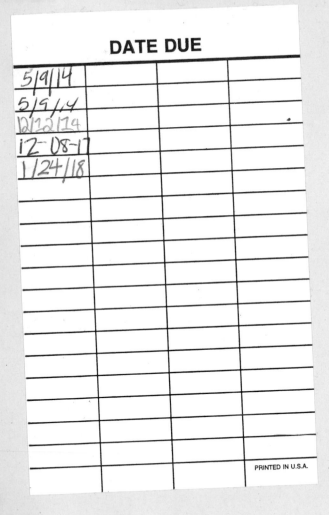

5/9/14			
5/9/14			
12/12/14			
12-08-17			
1/24/18			
			PRINTED IN U.S.A.